He stood a long time, staring down at her

Then almost negligently he bent toward her, caught her hands in his and with a savage jerk pulled her to her feet.

Her heart was hammering in a most unfamiliar way, and she had to bend backward to put as much distance between her face and his as was possible. Only the lower parts of their bodies were in close proximity; she was uncomfortably aware of his hands going around her waist, sliding down her hips as he molded her more closely against him. He smiled down at her for a moment and laughed aloud as she snapped her face sideways with an expression of distaste.

"Do you really think I'd allow you to make such a fool of me, Bianca?"

Books by Alexandra Scott

Harlequin Romances

These books may be available at your local bookseller.

For a free catalog listing all titles currently available, send your name and address to:

Harlequin Reader Service
2504 West Southern Avenue, Tempe, AZ 85282
Canadian address: Stratford, Ontario N5A 6W2

Love Comes Stealing

Alexandra Scott

Harlequin Books

**TORONTO • NEW YORK • LONDON
AMSTERDAM • PARIS • SYDNEY • HAMBURG
STOCKHOLM • ATHENS • TOKYO • MILAN**

Original hardcover edition published in 1983
by Mills & Boon Limited

ISBN 0-373-02585-8

Harlequin Romance first edition November 1983

Printed in U.S.A.

CHAPTER ONE

SUBCONSCIOUSLY approving, Bianca watched the striking young woman approach, and dispassionately admired the longish legs fashionably enclosed in brown cord knee breeches and ribbed stockings. The red fox jacket with the nipped-in waist had the collar turned up so that the golden glinting fur made a seductive frame for the glowing features. Features which, with a gasp of surprise and amusement as Bianca returned from her dream world to the noisy reality of the busy international airport, she saw every time she looked in a mirror.

The wide dark eyes, thickly fringed with long lashes, glanced about her in shamed embarrassment as if all the dallying crowds could see into her mind. And Bianca felt ridiculously relieved none showed the faintest suspicion that the attractive young woman had failed to recognise her own reflection.

The truth was, Bianca lingered by the mirror eyeing herself with a few surreptitious sidelong glances, she just wasn't used to the new-look Bianca Hill. Any more than she was used to jet-setting round the world with a first-class ticket. It was still hard to get used to the idea of being the new senior consultant (Europe) for a New York-based company.

It had been the best thing that could have happened when the internationally famous Fantasque Beauty Products had taken over the small company where she had worked for the last three years and now she had a job in the public eye and an image to maintain. And of course with the job went the money with which to help the image along.

Now with the generous dress allowance (non-taxable) on top of her salary, she was able to buy the fashionable clothes which were essential for the image Fantasque were anxious to promote. And her first trip to the States on business had provided an opportunity for an orgy of shopping, all as exciting and up to the minute as the clothes she was wearing and which had changed her appearance so radically.

Bianca moved on a little reluctantly. If she had followed her own inclination she would have stayed longer, admiring what she saw in the glass, noting again how the new range of colours just brought out for the autumn suited her. They might in fact have been designed with her in mind. All the soft glowing brownish shades went so perfectly with the intense gold-flecked brown of her eyes, and her skin tones seemed to cry out for the lip colours which ranged through apricot, rust and tawny pink and the stunningly gorgeous eye-shadows. The aubergine she was wearing, now so discreetly applied, she knew could look sensational in artificial light, if used blatantly.

A smile curved the corners of the wide mouth as she remembered how Joe Salinger had reacted at the dinner party which had been given by the company last night. She gave as much credit to Fantasque as to her own personality. More if she were being completely honest. She was sure she hadn't *that* much effect on men as a general rule, although she enjoyed flirting with them. And that, she would never have admitted as much to anyone but herself, was because she found it an effective means of protection, something to prevent them, and her, from taking their romantic advances seriously.

Now she was enjoying life too much, finding so much satisfaction in her new, demanding job, so much positive comfort in her new-found affluence that she had no thoughts of a permanent liaison. Marriage and children might, just *might*, lie some way off in the future, but at the moment she was more than happy with life as it was.

It hadn't always been like that. There had been a time, aeons ago when she had been little more than a child, when those abandoned dreams were exactly what she did have in mind. Just thinking about it now could cause her a little grimace of pain, even though she was long since over that. But she could never quite forget the anguish it had been at the time.

'Sorry.' A young man, bearded, wearing jeans and leather bomber jacket brushed accidentally against her and quickly apologised. 'I'm *sorry*.' His blue eyes widened in exaggerated admiration, white teeth fringed by the golden curling whiskers of the Norseman in a fairy story smiled at her, and he lagged behind his companions. Bianca flushed a little, hitched her leather travelling bag higher on to her shoulder, and saw his attention drawn to the tied-on destination label.

'You are going to London?' He registered extreme disappointment, disbelief. 'And I to Copenhagen.' He touched his fingers to his lips as he hurried after his friends, 'Parting is such sweet sorrow.'

The brief, unimportant encounter cheered Bianca, made her feel less alone and she watched him make his way to the far end of the hall where there was a group of similarly dressed young people, students presumably. But before she had time to do more than notice, the number of her own flight was called and she crossed at once to the departure lounge.

Still a relatively inexperienced traveller, she was one

of the first on board, finding herself in splendid isolation in the first class although the rest of the plane filled up quickly. But gradually, as departure time drew near, the more spacious first-class seats were taken up. It was a mild thrill to see an internationally-known pop star complete with his latest 'companion', an equally famous beauty and television personality, take up the vacant seats across the aisle and then a smooth looking Arab with a lovely American girl sat down directly in front of her.

Bianca looked at her watch and had just come to the comfortable conclusion that she was to have two seats to herself when there was a little stir behind her, a twittering from the stewardesses as they escorted the newcomer to his place and a briefcase was dropped on to the seat next to hers. At the same moment she decided she would be too hot in her fox jacket and, reluctant as she was to part with such a flattering garment, she thought she would do better without.

She rose, slipped it from her shoulders, reaching to tuck it into the overhead compartment and found herself relieved of the task.

'Let me help you.' The voice was deep brown, vibrant and vaguely known to her. It had a far-away familiarity which brought her eyebrows together in a frown of concentration, and less pleasantly a clammy feeling attacked her palms, discomfort fluttering in her chest.

'Thank you.' Her view of him was blocked by one of the stewardesses with whom he was involved in a tête-à-tête, very discreet so it was impossible without leaning obviously in their direction to hear what was being said. But she could see an immaculately-suited dark arm stretched overhead.

Bianca resumed her seat, smoothing down the apricot

silk of her cossack-style blouse, trying to find some reassurance in the warm softness of its loose elegance. Wondering with a distrait little shudder just why any reassurance should be necessary.

The man laughed as he sat down, looking up at the golden-haired girl who was so anxious about his well-being. Whisper, whisper she went and he laughed again. 'Very well, Freddie. That will be fine.'

'Will you please fasten your seatbelts. Fasten your seatbelts, please.' She went on her smiling way the length of the aircraft, exuding an air of complacent satisfaction which Bianca, following her progress, found very irritating. Without looking at him, Bianca was at least as much aware of the man by her side—he was much too large to ignore—and sensed that he too wore a smile of self-satisfaction as he settled and busied himself with his seatbelt.

Then almost at once her attention was diverted from what was happening inside the plane for the great machine was taxiing along the runway in preparation for take-off. This was always the time when she was nervous, those moments when it turned at the far end and you felt all the enormous power of the engines as sufficient thrust was developed to enable the machine to push itself away from the earth and to soar in some incredible fashion up into the sky. She never could believe it was possible and always closed her eyes and she did so now.

'It's all right.' The voice close to her ear was only slightly amused, more reassuring and considerate. 'We've been up for quite five minutes.'

A smile curved Bianca's lips and still lying back in her seat the thickly lashed eyes flicked open. Her head moved lazily on the soft cushion at her back, and there was a dreamy, expectant feeling as she turned to look at him, that earlier elusive fear had been forgotten. Now all her senses were quivering as she turned to view the man who was obviously so attractive to the gorgeous air stewardess, and whom she knew quite definitely she too, would find attractive.

The smile stayed on her face as if it had been painted there. Only her eyes went blank with shock. And he, allowing his glance to drift over her with the assurance of a connoisseur, did not trouble to hide his appreciation. 'It's the whine of the engines,' he went back to his subject. 'It takes some getting used to.'

'Yes.' Still she smiled, although inside she was as empty and bitter as a squeezed lemon. Then with an appearance of normality she sat up, rummaged in her handbag and brought out the book she had bought for the journey. It was a serious read, specially chosen so she wouldn't waste time with the trivial. With determination she opened it on page seven, smoothed back the leaves firmly, and looked down. Any other man's willingness to be dismissed would have been a disappointment, but now she was glad that he so quickly lost interest and applied himself to the sheaf of papers he had taken from his briefcase. The printed page blurred before her eyes and she was swept back down the dark corridor of memory.

She had been only eighteen when she had met Simon Percival. They had both hit the city at the same time, she having got her first job with a top London store selling cosmetics on one of their beauty counters, and Simon starting as a management trainee with the most famous multiple store in the country. When they had met, introduced by a girl who worked with Simon and lived in the same rather dreary block of bed-sits as Bianca, they had both been feeling a bit lonely—the excitement had begun to dim a little and they consoled each other.

It had seemed slightly daring when she had asked him back for a meal. Then she had panicked when she remembered all she had to cook on was a double gas burner in the large cupboard which was the kitchen. The hours she had spent poring over Katherine Whitehorn's book about cooking in a bed-sit!

In the end she had done just about the only thing she knew, a beef casserole which was fine with french bread and a tomato salad. For pudding they had had slices of cheesecake from Simon's store, then mugs of instant coffee. Even now she couldn't eat cheesecake without remembering.

The bed had been an embarrassment, filling, as it seemed on that first evening, the entire room. And it hadn't helped that you had to use it as a seat. How long had she spent debating? Would it be better to ask him to sit there? Or should she wave him to the only comfortable chair and sit on the bed herself? Suppose she were to relax a bit too much?—as they were having a bottle of red wine that seemed only too likely—and suppose she lay back in a moment of forgetfulness and he pounced on her!

Darling Simon. The idea didn't even cross his mind. His intentions were strictly honourable. So much so that he had asked her to marry him before they had known each other three months and she had accepted.

It would have been nicer if he had been more romantic, but it was sensible to think of things like finances. And it was true that with two salaries they could afford a much more attractive flat than they could individually.

'I don't mind if it's only one room, Bee,' his enthusiasm had been catching, 'but it must be a huge room, one we can breathe in, and with a decent kitchen and bathroom.'

'Mmm.' Bianca buried her face in his navy-striped waistcoat. 'But where are we going to find such a place, Simon?'

'Oh, we'll find one. I heard through one of our managers that there might be one going in Earl's Court. Rent controlled so it needs doing up, but we can use our own ideas. A few tins of paint and we could transform it.'

'I suppose there's a hundred others after it.'

'Don't be defeatist, darling. If you want a thing, go out and get it. That's my motto. After all, we've no one to please but ourselves.'

That was true enough. Bianca's parents were dead and her only sister, four years older than herself, was now working in Toronto. And Simon had only a father and stepmother who lived abroad and with whom he seemed to have lost both contact and interest. The only relative he ever spoke of with any feeling was someone he called Daniel, a mysterious second cousin once removed, who lived somewhere in Dorset. Bianca had the idea, she couldn't think where she had got it, that Daniel was a writer and that Simon held him in some respect, even a little trepidation.

'Yes, but . . .' Somehow the idea of a hole-and-corner marriage was not one that appealed to Bianca. 'What kind of wedding had you in mind, Simon?'

'Oh, register office. We can run along one morning and get the thing fixed up and arrange to meet some of the crowd in the pub for a drink to celebrate. You don't want a fuss,' he moved his arm slightly so he could look down into her face, 'do you, darling?'

And when he looked at her with that little boy lost expression, Bianca couldn't stop her heart flipping over. So she lied convincingly, 'No, of course I don't.'

Nevertheless she hadn't quite lost her head. She had waited until they were almost certain of the flat before she had allowed Simon to get the licence. It was the flat that decided them in the end. The couple who had the property and were now moving north had made it so attractive, quite different from the dreary, neglected place they had expected. You would hardly have known it was a basement, especially not from the back where it looked out on to a paved courtyard. On the evening they had called, the golden slabs glowed in the sunlight and it looked almost continental with the flower-filled pots that the girl had arranged round about and they had an old pub table, one of the round iron ones, painted white, together with a couple of chairs and they had been eating out there all summer. Or so the girl had told them—of course it might have looked entirely different in the winter, but Bianca never had the opportunity to find out.

Two days before the wedding had been planned to take place, they were giggling together as they tried to accommodate some of Simon's clothes in Bianca's already overfilled wardrobe. There had been a slight mix-up over the tenancy of the flat in Earl's Court, but they were promised they could have it in about three weeks' time and in the meantime they had chosen Bianca's flat as being the most conveniently situated. Her divan bed could, when you pulled a lever, convert into one that was almost a double and they wouldn't be there long enough to find out it was only half as thick when it was opened.

They had just stuffed the contents of two suitcases into the cupboard and dressing-table and were lying, helpless with laughter, their arms about each other, when some-one came knocking at the door. Knocking! That was a polite way of putting it. Banging—hammering—would have been closer to the truth. They had huddled close together for a moment, eyes suddenly wide open, hearts pounding.

'Stopped by the bell,' Simon laughed down at her and with a wink levered himself up and walked across to the hall. It wasn't really a hall, more a slice of corridor which had been sub-divided again to make a minute shower room and leave just enough space for the door of the flat to open.

She lay for a moment, hair tumbled about her shoulders, eyes gleaming with pleasure that Simon's presence always brought. It was incredible to think that in two days' time they would be married; they would be lying together on this bed—opened out, of course—and *really* together. The deep sentimental sigh was interrupted by the sound of raised voices. Simon's and another, deeper, much more forceful, which she didn't recognise.

With a realisation of the scene that would meet any visitor's eye, she began to push herself up from the bed. Fingers went up to restrain her tousled hair, but before she could do much to restore things, the door was pushed open and a man was in the room, filling it almost, and Simon, very much like a child caught out in some misdemeanour, was standing just behind.

The man's eyes, dark, scathing and contemptuous, had taken in every detail in a single searing glance: the girl sprawled across the bed in a way which left little to the imagination; drawers and doors open so that the contents burst squalidly out. The window which overlooked a local market was grimy—Bianca had meant to clean it tomorrow so that she and Simon could lie and see the moon rising over the rooftops. And there was a patch on one wall where a previous tenant seemed to have spilled something which had leached its way through subsequent coats of emulsion with dogged persistence.

When he had done the room over thoroughly he looked again towards the bed where Bianca still lay, stunned into immobility. She was just like the rabbit to his stoat, until Simon moved, that is, and her eyes were drawn to his in dumb appeal.

'This is Bee.' Bianca was such a weird name in those days and she had always shortened it radically, hoping that her friends might imagine she had been christened Beatrice or some such more commonplace name. 'Bee, this is Daniel Bohun. You've heard me speak of him.'

But Daniel Bohun had no intention, certainly not after that first assessing glance, of wasting his time on insignificant little nobodies who were clearly no better than they should be, because he turned away without as much as a sign of acknowledgement.

'I'd just like to know what the hell you think you're playing at, Simon.'

Simon swallowed nervously. Still half reclining on the bed, Bianca had known how he was feeling and she got up at once, crossed to where he was standing beside the intruder and slipped her hand through his arm. She looked defiantly up into the man's face hoping Simon was doing the same. If he was, the defiance didn't stretch to his voice which was a bit shaky, apologetic. 'Wh-what do you mean?'

'You know damn well what I mean.'

Bianca's heart was hammering uncomfortably but she found the courage to raise her chin a little and speak, determined this Daniel Bohun, the second cousin who wrote in Dorset she supposed, should not imagine that he was going to trample all over them.

'There's no need to use bad language,' she said coldly.

His attention flicked to her, then, with the same disdain he had shown earlier, back to her companion. 'I'm waiting, Simon,' he said menacingly.

'Well,' although she wasn't looking at him Bianca felt him shrug, 'the truth is, Bee and I have decided to get married.'

'*Bee* and you have decided.' The way he said it implied that it had been wholly her idea. Bianca trembled with anger as she looked into that handsome, callous face but before she could do anything like spit or kick him on the shins, he went on with what seemed a valid enough point. 'And didn't you think that maybe it was an important enough decision to let your family know?'

Again Simon shrugged but it was a moment before he answered. 'I didn't think Dad would be all that interested.'

'You must know that's not true.' Then, as if his exasperation was almost too much for him, he reached into his pocket and pulled out a case from which he extracted a cigarette which he lit with an expensive-looking lighter. In fact everything about him was expensive, from the lightweight summer suit the colour of burnt cream, the brown polo-neck sweater in a silky material, and the heavy gold watch on his wrist. The light flicked off, he drew smoke into his lungs, exhaled it in a sigh and walked across to look moodily out of the window.

Don't mind me, Bianca fumed at the arrogant back. I just live here, pay the rent, clean the place once in a while, you just go on with your smoking without even asking my permission—it doesn't matter that I'll have to breathe your foul fumes when I'm lying in bed tonight.

'And if it was true, then I would still have expected you to let me know. I am after all your Godfather, your guardian while your father is abroad.' He was a dark powerful shape against the window, even more intimidating than he had been.

'Yes, maybe I should have done that.' Simon's courage seemed to be reviving a little. 'But I am over age you know, Daniel.' There was even a hint of cockiness about him now, but that was almost instantly squashed.

'Over age!' The tone was scathing. 'You don't know what you're about. You're both kids.' For the first time he gave a fraction of his attention to Bianca. 'What about your family? Have they been invited to this . . . celebration?' The word was chosen deliberately to sound offensive and the girl found she was very much in the mood to take offence.

'I don't have any parents. My mother died when I was a child and my father was drowned in a bathing accident when I was sixteen.' She hoped that would put him in his place.

'And how long ago was that?'

'It was two years ago,' she said coldly.

'Then at eighteen you're too young to marry,' he said with brutal lack of sympathy for her position, 'especially when you have no relatives to advise you.'

'I have an older sister,' now contrarily she was anxious for him to know she wasn't entirely alone in the world, 'and she has no objection.' Not quite true because Cindy, in an unexpected telephone call from Toronto, had advised caution.

'More fool her.' The man stared at her for a moment then his fingers took the cigarette to his mouth again, paused, eyes narrowed against the curl of blue smoke, and flicked over her figure as if another, totally unwelcome idea had just occurred to him. 'For God's sake,' he ground out the words, 'don't tell me you're pregnant!'

Bianca felt herself go hot all over, she longed to cry, but in her determination not to, she relinquished her contact with Simon and took a step closer to the window. 'How like you,' she stormed. 'How like you with your sordid little mind to think such a thing. No,' the sob trembled in her throat as the tears did in her eyes, 'at least you can put your mind at rest on that point—I'm not pregnant.'

'Good.' He seemed not a whit put out by her attack, and simply stubbed out his cigarette in a pretty china dish she used for after dinner mints when Simon came round. 'In that case you'd better collect your things, Simon, and I'll take them back for you.'

The calm assumption of the man might have been funny. What stopped her laughing was her fear that Simon might do just what he was told. She glanced behind and saw his uncertainty, knew that he didn't know quite what to do. Some remnants of pride stilled her tongue, refused to let her plead as her heart begged her to do. Instead, she just stood there between the two men, her eyes wide and defensive but *willing* Simon to be defiant for once in his life.

But she had been without any real expectation that he would behave so uncharacteristically and when he came towards her, touched her on the arm and said haltingly, 'Maybe it would be best, Bee darling,' she hadn't even been particularly surprised.

Hurt, angry, humiliated, all of these, but not surprised. It was only long afterwards that it occurred to her that she should have been shocked. Surely the easy acquiescence of the man she had been going to marry ought to have been a bitter surprise and disappointment to her. He was the strong support she ought to have been able to lean on, the one on whom she should have been able to depend for all the warmth and comfort which marriage entails. Yet at the very first test he gave way and abandoned his plans. Surely she ought to have expected more of him and been surprised.

Instead, all the blame she had hung round Daniel Bohun's shoulders, like an albatross. In her mind Simon was like herself, an innocent victim; they both suffered while the architect of their unhappiness went on from strength to strength.

But immediately after the abandonment of their plans to marry, Simon was whisked north to complete his training in one of the firm's stores somewhere in the north-west of Scotland. In fact Bianca had seen him only once after that painful meeting with Daniel Bohun, and that she suspected was only because he had found he had left his briefcase with documents in the corner of her tiny dark hall. He had been waiting out on the landing when she returned tired and depressed from the store on the day that should have been her wedding day.

'I'm sorry about all this, you know that, darling.' He tried to put his arm round her and looked sulky when she moved away.

'Are you?' She looked at him levelly, annoyed that he refused to meet her eyes. 'Daniel Bohun must be a pretty important man.'

'Oh.' He looked momentarily perplexed. 'How do you mean, Beé?'

'I mean—' Unable to look at him any longer she turned and went to the window, still grimy she noticed, but she no longer had any urgent reason for perching outside to wash it. 'I mean, for him to arrange for you to be so immediately whisked away. Out of temptation's way.'

'Oh, that.' Simon's fair skin coloured. 'Well, I suppose he does know a lot of influential people. But . . . I hope you won't hold it against Daniel. He's only thinking of what's the best for us.'

'For you, maybe.' She hadn't known she had it in her to speak so coldly. 'I don't think he was much concerned with my feelings.'

'Oh well, he does know me . . .'

'I would have expected you, Simon, to fight a little harder for us. Not to cave in just as easily as you did.'

'Well, yes.' Simon looked so miserable and uncomfortable that if she hadn't been so unhappy herself she would have been unable to resist rushing across the room and throwing herself into his arms. 'But maybe it *is* for the best, Bee darling. We can think about it for a few months and then when I come back south we can have the kind of wedding you want, with your sister and some friends and . . .'

'It's hardly a month since you persuaded me against that. Don't expect me to believe that it's because of my wishes that you've changed your mind. Besides,' it was impossible to keep the bitterness out of her voice, 'if Daniel Bohun refuses to allow you to marry now, he's just as likely to do the same next time we decide.'

'Daniel's not like that. He won't stand in our way a second time, I know he won't. And if he tries to then I simply won't let him. Bee . . .' He threw down his briefcase, came towards her and this time Bianca did not move away from his comforting arms. She sobbed quietly against his chest for a few moments then allowed her eyes to be dried with his handkerchief and believed him when he said he would write every week.

And he did. For the first month at least. But then the letters stopped and gradually Bianca ceased even to expect them. It had helped a great deal that a small promotion had come her way. The store she worked with had opened a tiny parfumerie in one of London's top hotels and she had been offered the position. It had caused one or two raised eyebrows among the staff, but she had been happy enough to take it and gradually her affair with Simon had drifted to the back of her mind.

The only thing that revived the unhappy memory was the frequency with which the man she had come to hate appeared on television. It had begun about a year afterwards when casually pressing the knobs one evening in search of a diverting programme she had tuned in to a new programme on BBC 2.

'*Bias*', the anonymous voice had intoned solemnly, 'the programme you have been waiting for. *Bias*, where the brightest and best brains in public life today are given a platform to express their own *bias* to one particular aspect of everyday life. And here, to chair the programmes, to stamp them with his own brand of incisive questioning, is that well-known writer and broadcaster, Daniel Bohun.'

And there, Bianca in the act of taking a huge bite from an apple, paused, as the man she had vowed to hate all her life appeared in front of her, in the very room where he had trampled all her hopes and dreams in the dust. For a moment she had been too shocked and angry to speak. Then a bound took her to the set, a flick of the switch removed him from her sight, cut off the smooth, well-modulated tones in mid-sentence.

The satisfaction was fleeting. For much of the evening she walked up and down the floor, trying to control the misery which the sight of him had unleashed. Hours later she saw the apple, one bite removed from its green crispness now scarred and brown, no longer appetising. Numbly she dropped it into the waste bin under the kitchen sink, slowly undressed and went to bed.

In the intervening years he had appeared more and more on the television. Bianca found increasing satisfaction in using the off switch whenever his face threatened her peace of mind. In fact, everything about him became a bit of a phobia with her, so much so that the friend with whom she now shared a flat expressed the opinion that she was trying to deny the attraction she undoubtedly felt for him. Which couldn't have been further from the truth. Recently she had heard his name mentioned in connection with breakfast television, but the only effect that had was to confirm her opinion that television before six p.m. was immoral.

'Could I offer you a drink?' The voice of Daniel Bohun by her side couldn't be ignored and Bianca lifted her eyes from the book in her hands. Subconsciously she noticed that she was now at page thirty but she knew she hadn't read a single word.

She turned her head in his direction to give him the briefest of smiles, one that could not be mistaken for encouragement by even the most hardened womaniser, which the gossip columns proved him to be. 'No, thank you.' She held his eyes for a cool minute, and then returned her own to the top of page thirty-one, convinced that nothing about her had betrayed the hammering pulses, the clammy hands.

In that moment when they had looked at each other she had sensed a stirring in the veils of recollection as if something warned him that this was not his first encounter with this girl. But, a smile of confidence turned her lips faintly upwards, he would never recognise her, not in a hundred years.

He had seen her just that once, whereas she had seen him dozens of times, and dozens of times had watched him disappear into a tiny dot on the television screen. And over the years she had changed much more than he.

She had shed half a stone for one thing. It had been a struggle, but now she had done it, her new slimness was easy to maintain. And when she had known Simon she had been experimenting with some new hair colourings which the store had been promoting and had then been a not very subtle blonde. The thought of that wild artificial colour made her shudder now, but just for a few weeks she had enjoyed it and the whole range of unsuitable shades with which she had tried to alter her skin colourings. So, there was no use Daniel Bohun racking his brains, the girl sitting next to him was not the naïve teenager he had known, she had gone for ever—destroyed by him! It was a dramatic thought which brought a prick of tears to her eyes.

It wasn't the most comfortable journey she had ever had, sitting next to a man to whom she had just given a polite, maybe not so polite brush-off, while munching her way through the first-class menu. The smoked salmon was just a bit salty, but having refused a drink with such firmness she had to wait till the coffee came round before having her thirst quenched. From the corner of her eye she could see the half bottle of Verdicchio which he had chosen and she even wondered if he had placed it purposely where it could taunt her.

And it was aggravating that he didn't seem unduly disappointed by her unfriendliness. Nor lonely, because first one of the stewardesses came and stood beside him, then the other, so that Bianca was the one who felt excluded. Even the pilot had a special word for such a special passenger, it helped that she could be sarcastic, and the two men chatted like old friends till the pilot, remembering his duty, leaned over to ask Bianca if she was enjoying her journey.

Nevertheless, it had been a relief when she recognised the coastline of England beneath them and she could begin to get ready for the descent. She took advantage of his temporary absence to get her jacket down from the upper compartment so that when he returned, she was ready for disembarkation, dressed in her gorgeous red fox jacket, hair and make-up immaculate, gloved hands holding on to her handbag as if someone might snatch it from her and her eyes fixed very firmly on the scenery outside.

The glass gave a reflection and she saw his glance rest briefly on her in the moment before he took his seat, but she wasn't certain if she really saw the slight smile, the faint shrug as if here was a woman whom even he couldn't understand. On the whole, she decided with absolute fairness, that might have been a figment of her rather bitchy imagination. Only it irritated her as much as if it had been proved.

When she reached the tarmac she heaved a sigh of relief and even smiled at the attractive young American girl who was walking, fingers linked, with the Arab. She had left Daniel Bohun in the aircraft where she imagined he and the stewardess were involved in complicated arrangements which would give pleasure to both of them. It was a positive joy to allow her imagination to run riot.

It was only when she was approaching the main building that she became aware of the crowds of photographers milling round the entrance, cameras at the ready. They were jostling each other for positions, peering and stretching to catch sight of the passengers who were coming along the corridors.

Of course, Bianca reminded herself with a little smile. She had had to push past a mass of guitars in the aisle of the plane. They must be waiting to take shots of Monty Verdi. Pop stars were always news in the tabloids, especially when they deny rumours of romance with anyone as famous as Ginny Forsyth. Now, it looked as if patience was to be rewarded and they would get the shots that would send them happily back to their editors.

Bianca didn't look round when she heard footsteps hurrying behind her; she had no reason to think they would concern her and in any case by this time her mind was way ahead of her, wondering how long it would take for the luggage to come through and how long she would have to wait before she could pick up a taxi.

She had almost reached the exit and the excited group of photographers when she felt a hand on her arm, a voice which she knew only too well spoke to her, and she turned to look disdainfully into the eyes of Daniel Bohun, ignoring the book he was holding out towards her.

'I saw this when I was picking up my briefcase.' His expression was as formal as his words. 'It had slipped down the side of your seat and I realised that you had forgotten it.'

There was a hint of something in his dark eyes that angered Bianca, more than the anger she normally felt for him. Perhaps it was the sense that deep down he was amused by her behaviour, the idea that he wasn't prepared to take her too seriously, as if he was telling her that all that long-ago pain, caused by him, endured by her, was less than nothing.

Behind her she heard the murmur of the waiting newsmen and suddenly into her mind came this priceless idea. She didn't know if it would work but it was well worth a try. And Daniel Bohun's face was at least as well known as Monti Verdi's.

Her hand went up in an imperious little gesture which was guaranteed to give the onlookers the impression that she was being annoyed. Her face was cold with disdain and she made certain that her voice was clear enough to travel.

'Please, would you stop pestering me.' And ignoring the book she swept past him while ahead of them flash bulbs popped.

And that, she thought, as she walked with a wholly assumed air of self-assurance towards the luggage carousel, that, Mr Daniel Bohun, is just a small, a very small repayment for all the unhappiness you caused to two innocent young people.

CHAPTER TWO

BIANCA was lying with her back on the floor, legs extended at right angles up the wall. She was reading a magazine and munching an apple when the door opened and Elspeth Lewin came into the hall of the flat they shared.

'What on earth . . .?' Elspeth surveyed her flat-mate in amazement before dropping her packages on the floor and herself into the only available chair while she fanned herself with the *Evening Clarion*.

'Hi!' Bianca waved a hand in the direction of her friend. 'Busy day?'

'Busy!' Elspeth sighed pathetically. 'I just wish I worked for the kind of firm that gives days off to recover from jet lag.'

'But you haven't got it.' Bianca returned to her magazine and her apple. 'So how can you expect a day off for it?'

'By the look of you, you haven't got it either.' Elspeth levered herself out of the chair and turned in the direction of the kitchen. 'Would you like a cup of tea?'

'I'll get it.' With a lithe move Bianca uncurled herself from her position and moved across the floor. 'It's all ready and the kettle's been boiling.'

'Thanks. I need a bit of pampering.' Elspeth kicked off her shoes behind the kitchen door and leaned wearily against the wall while she watched the other girl's deft movements.

'I think all this talk of jet lag is so overrated. I don't feel especially tired today. Exhilarated rather.'

'That's just about how you look.' Elspeth accepted the cup that was held out to her. 'I hope that leotard isn't only to make me realise how overweight I am.'

'Of course not. You have a marvellous figure. You know that and I'm not going to flatter your ego by keeping on about it. Anyway, I've got another of these leotards, not in brown but in navy with scarlet round the cuffs, you can have it if you like.' She surveyed her friend's peaches and cream complexion over the rim of her cup. 'It's more your colour than mine.'

'Oh no. Thanks, Bianca. I've no intention of struggling into a leotard and doing horrible exercises. All I want to do when I get home is relax. What was that you were up to out there?'

'It was just this article.' Bianca nodded towards the magazine tossed down on the sink top. 'I was reading about how it does you good to lie with your feet against a wall. Sends all the blood to your heart, it says here,' she squinted down at the paper. 'Anyway you ought to know all about that. Or doesn't the modern medical secretary know about these things?'

Elspeth giggled. 'I know more about bunions and varicose veins than about beauty therapy. You're the resident expert on all that kind of nonsense.'

'I don't think any of them do a pennyworth of good.' Bianca sighed. 'In fact, if all the promises you read in advertisements for beauty products were genuine, how come there are so many people dissatisfied with their looks?'

'You'd better not let Fantasque hear you saying that,' Elspeth moved across to the cooker so she could refill her cup, 'otherwise there won't be any more first-class trips across the Atlantic for you.' She paused, 'Is it back to the grind again tomorrow, Bianca?'

'What? Oh, yes, I suppose so. But thank goodness I've a day off on Friday. Did I tell you I'm going down to Cindy's?'

'Yes, you said. Well you can't keep making excuses can you?'

'No. And I don't want to. After all she's the only relation I have. But it's awkward when you really can't stand your brother-in-law.'

'Well, from what you say she's happy enough. That's what counts.'

'I suppose so. Only I can't, I just *can't* understand what she saw in him. Oh, he's loaded of course. At least he seems to be. But he's so much older than Cindy. And I always get the impression that he's on the fiddle, not actually dishonest but . . .'

'Well, these kinds of people often are. Gambling and gaming, it isn't the kind of business that really inspires confidence. Still, I'm sure most of them are honest. I thought you said something about a record company.'

'Oh, he talks about all kinds of things. He seems to know a lot of people in showbiz, drops names a lot. Oh, it's so many things. I think maybe I'm unfair to him because when I first met him he had a wife and family and yet he was going about with Cindy.'

'I would have thought that was her fault as much as his. After all, she was his secretary and bound to know.'

'Oh yes, I'm not blaming him entirely. And to be truthful he's always especially nice to me, goes out of his way to make me feel at home.'

'Well, I shouldn't worry about them. She was old enough to know her own mind and what she wanted out of life.'

'Mmm. I often wonder if that's why she married him. She was twenty-nine after all and I think was beginning to wonder . . . You remember I told you she got engaged when she was in Canada, then she came home and it was a while before she got herself straightened out.'

'What happened to him do you think? The one in Canada?'

'She never really said. Just that it didn't work out. Anyway,' firmly Bianca applied herself to the washing-up, 'I'll go down this weekend and then I needn't go again for a while. I'm sure she'll try to persuade me to go down at Christmas but three or four days of Lex will be just too much for me, so I'll just have to try to think of some excuse. Now you go and have your bath first, then I'll have one. I'm going to treat you to a meal out tonight. I still have some cash from economising on my expenses while I was in New York. We'll try that little Italian place on the corner of Charles Street, shall we?'

It was almost time to go and Bianca was just putting the finishing touch to her eyes when a yell from the sitting-room sent her hurrying through brush still poised.

'Good heavens.' Bewildered she looked across to where Elspeth was peering at something in the newspaper she was holding in her hand. 'I thought at the very least you'd laddered your tights.'

'Bianca . . .' The face Elspeth turned for a second in Bianca's direction was flushed and accusing. 'Bianca, you dark horse . . . It is, isn't it?' She frowned as uncertainty chased the excitement from her features and in that moment Bianca suddenly knew just what was causing such interest.

'What is?' she asked with incredible coolness and

turned back towards the door until her friend's tone stopped her.

'Bianca, don't you dare sneak away.' Elspeth, who could be formidable when she chose, now strode across the room, shaking the page in Bianca's direction. 'And don't tell me that isn't you because I know otherwise.'

'What?' Bianca said weakly as she took the sheet and glanced down as if what it contained could be of no possible interest to her.

'You know perfectly well what. I wasn't sure at first but now I am. Guilt is written on your face for anyone to see. You might have told me.' With a sudden change of mind she took back the newspaper which she had just thrust into her friend's hands and read in a sardonic headline voice, '"Just who is the titian-haired beauty who gave Daniel Bohun such a decisive brush-off yesterday?"' Elspeth's laugh showed her white even teeth then she continued, '"Daniel Bohun had what must have been an unusual experience yesterday at London Airport. He came rushing along a corridor after a most attractive mystery woman who appeared anxious to have nothing to do with the well-known man-about-town. In fact she was heard quite distinctly to request that he should stop pestering her. As our picture illustrates only too clearly, Mr Bohun did not take this request kindly!"'

'Let me see.' Bianca's cheeks were pink as she snatched the paper from her friend and looked down at the photograph. Her first feeling was one of dismay. To be so prominently featured in a trashy gossip column was not what she had had in mind when the idea had flashed into her head. She had thought only to make him look a little small in front of a group of Nosey Parker photographers. But if, she studied the picture closely, if that was what she had wanted then she had succeeded beyond her expectations.

In the picture Daniel Bohun was easily identifiable although it was seldom he was 'caught' with such a silly expression on his face. The hand holding her book was obscured by her body, and her own face, half turned from the cameras, was less easy to recognise. Of course, anyone who knew her well might be able to pick her out, and it hadn't been too hard for Elspeth who had seen what she was wearing when she had arrived home.

'How could you, Bee?' Elspeth's voice, now that she had joined her friend in a study of the picture, was admiring, incredulous, regretful, all of these. 'And all this time I've been thinking you were harbouring a secret yearning for the man.' She sighed. 'How could you do it, Bianca? You've made him look so silly.'

'Oh, it wasn't quite as bad as it looked,' Bianca lied. 'You know they can twist things to suit themselves.'

'But,' Elspeth took up the paper Bianca had discarded, 'you must have been speaking to him, saying something. Surely they didn't make this up completely.' She read again. '"She was heard quite distinctly to request that he should stop pestering . . ." Did you actually say that, Bianca?'

'Something like that.' Bianca blushed. 'It won't do him any harm you know. People like that, in the public eye, lap up any kind of publicity.'

'I don't know . . . Daniel Bohun isn't exactly . . .'

'Of course he is, Elspeth.' Returning confidence made Bianca speak briskly. 'There aren't many weeks when he doesn't feature in articles of one kind or another. It will do him all the good in the world to be taken down a peg or two.' Firmly now she walked to the door and a moment later was surveying her reflection in the mirror.

'You realise, of course,' Elspeth poked her head round the bedroom door, 'that I could make a small fortune if I were to give the *Clarion* the tip-off.'

'What do you mean?' Bianca looked blank.

'I mean, they call you a mystery woman. I'm sure they would give a lot of money to find out who you are.'

Bianca's eyes widened in dismay. 'Don't you dare, Elspeth.' Then when her friend's head disappeared she followed her to the door. 'Don't you *dare*, Elspeth!' she yelled at the bathroom door but all the reply was the sound of laughter and a running tap. The thought of not only the *Clarion* and its millions of readers discovering her identity, but of Daniel Bohun finding out the name of the girl in the photograph, was just too awful to be borne.

'Elspeth,' she pleaded as her friend reappeared.

'Of course not. Idiot.'

Bianca relaxed.

It was a trying railway trip to East Bredley in Kent with two changes then a bus journey, unless someone managed to meet her at the railway terminus. As a rule it suited Bianca, that being one of her excuses for making the effort so seldom, but today it was even more of a drag than usual as the jet lag was making a deliberate attempt to catch up with her.

Thus it was when she found her brother-in-law waiting to pick her up at the station her greeting to him was warmer than the one he was used to.

'Hello, Bianca.' The dark eyes always had a wary expression when they were dealing with her, but he relaxed a shade when she allowed him to brush her cheek with his lips. 'Mmm.' He held her away, approving the same outfit she had worn for her flight. 'It's obviously doing you good. You look a real swinger.'

'Thanks.' She refused to let him see how the expression grated but turned in relief to the large limousine, grateful that she needn't clamber on to the bus which was waiting to collect passengers from the next two trains then stop at every halt between here and the house. 'How are things, Lex?' Once he had nosed the car out of the station yard she sat back in her seat and looked at him. 'Haven't you been at the office today?'

'Oh,' he shrugged, massive shoulders under closely-fitting grey suiting, 'the recession you know.' His grin was, she decided, a trifle forced. 'People just don't have the money these days for enjoying themselves. So, as business is slack, I decided I could afford to take a day off. No use in flogging myself to death if there's no customers about, is there?'

'I see.' Bianca felt the old uneasiness sweep over her. No matter when she saw Lex, during his wildly prosperous spells or the times like now when he seemed less secure, she was always beset by uneasiness. 'Well,' she said comfortingly, 'they say we've reached the bottom and things will start to go up again soon.'

'Sure.' He handled the car with expert aggression which seemed part of his character. 'Now tell me about you? How was America?'

'Oh, I loved it. It was everything you said it would be Lex.' She could see that her words pleased him for at their last meeting he had waxed very enthusiastic about New York and had even hinted that he might break with all his UK interests and emigrate to where the opportunities were so much greater.

They were turning into the drive of the huge modern house before Bianca remembered that she hadn't even asked about Cindy. She had spoken to her on the telephone the previous night of course, and there was no point in asking Lex how she was when at this moment Cindy was opening the front door and coming down the short flight of steps.

'Go on,' the car came to a smooth halt, 'your sister has some news for you.'

But it wasn't till they had gone upstairs and were in the bedroom which Bianca always occupied on her brief stays that Cindy told her sister that she was expecting a baby.

'Cindy, how marvellous. I've been dying to become an auntie.' And she put her hands about her sister's shoulders and kissed her.

'Well,' Cindy looked a bit embarrassed, 'I'm glad someone is pleased.' She shrugged. 'I'm not certain Lex is. Not entirely,' she amended loyally.

'Oh, he will be,' Bianca assured her with all the confidence that lack of experience breeds. 'When he gets used to the idea.'

'I hope so. Only,' Cindy sank down onto the bed and twisted the huge diamond engagement ring she wore, 'I have to remember this isn't the first time for him. When you've been through it all before I suppose it loses some of its appeal. And this isn't a good time, he has some business worries.'

'Well, that's natural enough. Everyone has them at the moment. Or haven't you heard of the recession?' she joked.

'It's a bit more than that, but I'm sure we'll pull out of it.' With a determined effort she smiled and got up. 'We've been through difficult times before and I'm sure we will be again. Anyway, I did tell you we're having a slightly wild party tonight. Lex has some people coming he wants to impress so you'll do your best, won't you, love?'

'Of course.' Bianca determined to try and cheer her sister up. 'And I brought an outfit which will be sure to attract attention.'

'I knew I could depend on you.' This time the smile was more relaxed. 'It does me good to see you, Bee. I only wish you would come down more often, it would be so nice if we saw more of each other.'

'Well, you know how it is. I usually work on a Saturday and that makes the weekends so short. And you never seem to come up to town these days. Now tell me, what do you want? A boy or a girl? Might be better to have one of each in case Lex refuses to allow you to have any more.'

But when she returned to her room after having some tea downstairs, Bianca felt all her artificial good spirits evaporate. There was something more than Lex's usual ups and downs of business troubling both of them. Lex, who normally never smoked at all, had been lighting one cigarette after another while he drank cup after cup of tea and ate nothing. Cindy had kept watching him with an anxious expression which he noticed and which obviously irritated him.

Bianca sighed as she walked into her bathroom, turned on the hot water and watched the pale green marble bath fill up. If luxury had been what Cindy was after when she married then she had been successful. But surely a little less luxury and some more peace of mind would have been much more comfortable in the long run. She sighed again, and began to undo the buttons of her blouse as she went back into her bedroom.

Later, as she walked downstairs, Bianca paused on

the half-landing where she had a perfect view of herself in the long mahogany-framed mirror. She would never have believed that someone with her colouring could wear this rich, intense ruby red. The saleswoman in the shop on Fifth Avenue which dealt exclusively in couturier clothes at greatly reduced prices had almost begged her to try it on.

'You'll be just so sorry if you don't.' Her ripe Jewish New York contralto had been as persuasive as the bright smile and when Bianca had slipped into the garments she had been forced to blink once or twice. Then to admit that the saleswoman had been very perceptive.

She made the same admission now as she eyed herself in the red matador pants, the ridiculous, irresistible frilled mini-skirt belted with a broad cummerbund and the top, dolman sleeved and in a slightly paler shade. She had thought it absurd when it had been produced in the shop, and it was—absurd, extravagant, preposterous but exactly right for one of Lex's not very wild parties. And more important, exactly right for Bianca Hill. It did all sorts of things for her ego. She must watch that, she decided, as she wiped the satisfaction from her face and went downstairs sedately—her ego was receiving so many boosts these days that it was in danger of over-inflation.

The lower floor of the house was softly illuminated with light spilling from the gorgeous lamps dotted here and there. There were slits of concealed lighting drawing attention to special features in the hall; one behind a small pool and rock garden and several spotlights discreetly pointing up Lex's discerning taste in modern art. There was a hum of conversation from the drawing-room as Bianca crossed the deep carpeting and she wondered with a vague little spark of interest if there was any chance of meeting anyone she liked. On the whole she thought not. It was unlikely that she would find any of Lex's friends particularly attractive, and she shuddered a little. The very idea.

Lex spotted her straight away and came forward, his eyes warmly admiring, all evidence of anxiety swept away for the moment. He held a glass of champagne in one hand and with the other lifted one from a tray carried by one of the girls hired for the evening, offering it to his sister-in-law with a slight bow.

'Am I allowed to say how beautiful you look tonight, my dear?' He raised his glass in a faint salute then sipped.

'Of course. I never forbid remarks like that.'

'You are the kind of woman who improves with age, Bianca.'

'Oh, don't say that.' Her eyes drifted away from his, looking for her sister.

'Why not, most women would be pleased.'

'I don't know why I said it.' She caught sight of Cindy and prepared to move on. 'I suppose it made me feel like an antique. Or a bottle of wine, perhaps. I want to be at my best now. Right this minute.' She was surprised to find herself speaking so foolishly with Lex, even fishing for compliments.

'You will be at your best,' he responded with more gallantry than she was used to, 'for many years, Bianca.' But at the same time he gave the impression of having lost a little interest, as his eyes were on the open doorway through which he could see the wide hall and Bianca assumed he was looking for one of his important guests.

For the next half hour she was kept busy, greeting many of the people whom she had already met, and one or two whose names were vaguely familiar and whom she assumed were in the entertainment business. It was a fairly well-mixed crowd, most of them ordinary people living in the neighbourhood, if the residents of Lancing Lane could ever be called ordinary. There was the odd stockbroker, the head of one of the nationalised industries, a Euro-MP with his secretary, Bianca noted, not the wife who had been with him when she had met him last. Although the question hovered on her lips, she couldn't quite pluck up courage to ask him how she was.

Her back was turned to the door and she was bending her head to try to hear what someone was saying. It was a question from a striking-looking woman with dazzling white hair and black, black eyebrows; a question, Bianca gathered that had something to do with the outfit she was wearing. And she was just gathering breath to explain above the din how she had found it when she felt a touch on her arm and looked up into her sister's apologetic face.

'Would you excuse us, Diana?' Cindy apologised. 'Lex has someone he wants Bianca to meet.'

They threaded their way through the crowd, away from the huge window where Bianca had been standing, towards the door.

Bianca had a moment's impression of a tall figure, back turned towards her but it was an outline she would have recognised in her sleep. Her mind seemed to go completely blank, panic mounted in her, and she prayed for the ground to open and consume her completely, for a thunderbolt to come down from heaven and burn her to a crisp. But before those comparatively pleasant means of escape offered themselves, Lex caught sight of her, reached out a hand and pulled her to his side.

'And I'd like to introduce you to my sister-in-law.

Bianca, this is Daniel Bohun. And Daniel, this is Cindy's sister—Bianca Hill.'

Bianca held out her hand as if she were in a dream. Only she saw the way his eyes narrowed for a second before he reached out a hand to take hers. And his voice was as urbane and assured as ever when he answered:

'Now what a curious coincidence, Lex. You see, Miss Hill and I have already met.' He paused and his glance covered her with assumed admiration. 'And more than once.'

'You've met?' There was incredulity in Lex's voice, in the eyes which darted a series of glances from his important guest to his sister-in-law and back again. 'But how absolutely astonishing. You've never spoken of it, my dear.' She was oblivious of the warm smile in her direction, unaware too of how the surprise in Lex's expression quickly gave way to something different, infinitely more assessing. And that was because she was finding it impossible to look anywhere other than into the face of the man for whom she had such a consuming, such a very satisfying hatred.

It was the appearance of the beautiful girl at the top of the stairs which caused the diversion, made Bianca drag her eyes away from his. She turned with the others and watched the girl, who was instantly recognisable as the stewardess, come slowly down the long, angled stairway.

There was a faint smile on the girl's face as if she were only too well aware of the impression she was creating. Indeed it would have been difficult for anyone to be unconscious of the eyes watching, of the hush that had fallen momentarily on the group standing just outside the door of the drawing-room.

Freddie, Bianca even remembered her name, was

dressed in black, a sleek black that covered her from toe to the top of the high neckline; a fiercely modest, undeniably sexy dress, designed to cause piercing jealousy in any woman who saw it. The emotion stabbed through Bianca and without realising what she was doing she sent a quick glance in the direction of Daniel Bohun. He was watching the girl he had brought with him, a faint admiring smile on the normally cool lips as he appraised the spill of golden hair about her shoulders, the contrast between the black, faintly iridescent material and the pale beauty of the girl's features.

Too late, Bianca realised she had been caught in her secret observation. Blood drained from her face as she was subjected to his examination, and she saw the deliberate obliteration of his smile as he turned his eyes in her direction.

She was grateful that Cindy chose that moment to introduce her sister to the girl, relieved when she knew that the girl had not recognised her. So, she's stupid as well as beautiful, she thought, with bitchy satisfaction. Well, that should just about suit Daniel Bohun and she turned with a sudden enthusiasm back to the room where she could find the stockbroker who had been lengthily boring her on the exchange rates.

For the next two hours Bianca kept her distance from Daniel Bohun and his companion simply by throwing herself into the role of assistant hostess. Although there wasn't any real need, she bustled out and in the kitchen, insisting on washing up a tray of glasses when one of the hired helpers brought them in, adding touches to the platters of delicious food.

But this too brought problems, for each time she emerged she had to check that the coast was clear in case she blundered accidentally into Bohun's arms. When she was actually in the drawing-room she kept the maximum amount of space between them, although it was amazing how often, even with all her precautions, their eyes seemed to meet. He and Lex were involved in a fairly serious conversation and once when she looked up, she could have sworn that Daniel Bohun had his gaze rivetted on the top of her head. She had blushed, turned swiftly away and when she looked again both men had gone. Bianca assumed with a sigh of sheer relief that they had gone to Lex's study where they could continue their business discussions in comparative peace.

The buffet supper was served from the large table in the dining-room, where candlelight gleamed softly on polished silver and crystal. The whole scene looked very pleasant, Bianca decided, with groups of people sitting round the room, chatting while they ate. And Cindy had produced some gorgeous flower arrangements, all cream, pale yellow and dark green which contrasted beautifully with the highly polished mahogany.

When it was obvious that everyone was served, Bianca took an empty salad bowl and went to have it refilled in the kitchen. On her way she caught a glimpse of Freddie, tucked away in a corner with a young man more than ready to be dazzled. Thank goodness, she thought, as she walked across the deserted hallway, I hope he'll keep her out of my hair until Daniel Bohun comes back.

She was just reaching the kitchen door when the sound of voices through the opening study door made her put a spurt on. She just managed to escape in time, allowing the door to swing closed behind her, then listening as Lex led his visitor in the direction of the dining-room. She must be careful. If she returned now with the bowl full of lettuce she might be forced to offer it to him. As she refilled the dish, she frowned over the problem till one of the women solved it for her.

'Give that to me, Miss Hill. I'm going back with this mayonnaise.'

Bianca hung about for five minutes before she dared go out and when she did she positively tiptoed a few steps before she stopped with her head on one side. She would go upstairs and waste a few minutes redoing her make-up. She had taken a step towards the staircase when an arm shot out and grasped her by the wrist. Startled, heart hammering against her ribs, she looked up at him, eyes wide with fear.

'You and I, Miss Hill, have one or two things to discuss,' he ground the words out at her. Then before she could open her mouth to protest they were inside the small study, and he was leaning against the closed door with a look of immutable confidence and superiority while his fingers were still closed about her wrist like metal vises.

CHAPTER THREE

TIME seemed to be suspended while they glared at each other. At least Bianca glared, or tried to although it was difficult when the imminent crushing of her wrist bones threatened to bring the tears rolling down her cheeks. And the expression in his eyes was more condescending dislike than a glare. But she was forced to speak first, if only to spare herself the horror of crushed limbs.

'You're hurting me.' She tried to speak coldly but firmly, only her voice was less firm than she intended.

'Good.' He was pitiless but at least he released her, and watched with a certain cool satisfaction as she rubbed her wrists to emphasis his brutality.

'Will you move away from that door?' she asked with more hope than expectation. 'There are things I want to do in the kitchen.'

'And yet,' he jeered, 'you were planning to do a rush upstairs when I invited you to this little chat.'

'I wouldn't have thought you'd have to force women to speak to you. Not with your reputation.'

'We haven't come in here to discuss my reputation, rather . . .'

'Oh, I wonder how I got the idea that that's what we were going to discuss.' It helped her to jeer a little. 'Just how your reputation as a ladies' man was damaged by that silly photograph in the *Clarion*.'

'I'm glad you admit it was silly. But I presume that was the effect you wanted. But no, it wasn't that I wanted to speak about. If I got upset every time I figured in some

44

gossip column then I would need a psychiatrist. What . . .'

'How smug you sound.'

He continued as if she hadn't interrupted. 'What I wanted to say first of all was I'm sorry I didn't recognise you at once when we met on the plane.' His eyes drifted over her with a very expert, faintly surprised expression. 'You've changed. You must know that.' Suddenly he levered himself away from the door, and walked across to the desk as if there were no longer any danger of her escaping. She watched with narrowed, slightly suspicious eyes, struck by the graceful athletic way he moved, forced to admit that the cameras had done nothing to exaggerate the forceful presence of the man, nor to flatter his unconventional good looks.

There was little of the matinée idol about him, his features were too strong, too forceful for that. The hair which when she had last seen him had been a glossy but intense black was softened now by the merest touch of silver at the temples. Improved with age, Lex's phrase returning to her seemed appropriate till with a little thrill of displeasure she forced it away from her—approving thoughts were out as far as he was concerned.

Yet she could not force her eyes away. She watched as he helped himself from an engraved silver box to one of Lex's cigars and flicked a light to the tip. Then as he drew the smoke deep into his lungs he lounged easily against the edge of the desk, long legs crossed at the ankles, arms folded comfortably across his chest, and his eyes came up again to encounter hers.

'You caused me a sleepless night, Bianca.' Something deep inside her stirred as she heard him for the first time use her name. 'Do you know that?' Amusement lightened the deep voice, but no matter how she tried she could find no confirmation of it in his features. The mouth was as firm, as dispassionate as ever.

Briefly, without answering, she shook her head. Then, for a reason she could not understand, allowed herself to sink into a chair conveniently close to her. With a desire to appear at ease she allowed one arm to drape over the back of the chair, stretched her legs in front of her and smiled with what she hoped was condescending patience.

'Yes, all that night I wondered who you were.' Once again a long slow glance approved her. 'I knew we hadn't met recently, for quite frankly you were not the kind of girl I would have forgotten.' He noticed her slow blush, and something sparked in his dark eyes which intensified her response. He paused long enough for Bianca to become aware of her own hurried breathing, something which she was determined to control. 'And then, quite suddenly, when I was shaving next morning, something in my memory clicked. I remembered exactly when we had met. And in what circumstances.'

Recollection of the pain she had suffered then suffused Bianca. 'What do you expect me to say?'

His eyes narrowed a shade and the smile that had hovered at his mouth a moment earlier was no longer there. 'Perhaps I expect you to say thank you. But I'm sure you would think it's too much.' There was a faint hardening of his manner.

'You are so right.' Bianca moved smoothly, aggressively, as she got up from her chair and crossed towards him, anger flashing in her eyes. She felt better when she remembered why she hated him so much. 'Why should I thank you for spoiling my life?'

'Spoiling?' He raised one dark eyebrow. 'I shouldn't have thought I had done that. At least not permanently.

You look to me as if you have a great deal going for you. Obviously you've got a good job. You look good.' The dark eyes drifted over her meaningfully. 'Most people would think you have it made.'

'I'm not most people,' she hissed. 'I'm me. You came between me and something I wanted pretty badly. Don't expect thanks for that.'

'In spite of the fact that the years—' he frowned, '—how many is it, five, six?—have been so kind to you?'

'It's nearly eight.' The words were out before she could stop him.

'Ah, yes,' he nodded. 'That's right.' He frowned over some silent calculation. 'You were . . . So now, you must be twenty-six.'

'Nearly,' she snapped.

'Ah well, give or take a month or two. You look less,' he added patronisingly. 'But it is eight years ago, because Simon's eldest child is almost seven.'

Bianca, stunned by the blatant cruelty of the information, reached towards the desk for support, wondering vaguely why his features were swimming in front of her. She saw his hand come out towards her, found her senses again and withdrew a step.

'I suppose you want me to thank you for that information as well.'

'No.' His eyes searched her face with disturbing intensity, maybe even with a flicker of concern. 'I agree that would be too much. Only,' he hesitated, 'I shouldn't let it bother you. Not now.'

'Why?' It was a controlled shout. 'Why shouldn't I let it bother me? I *do* have feelings you know. I'm sorry if you find it difficult to understand.'

'What I'm trying to say,' if she had been in a fit state to notice she might have thought he had lost a little assurance, 'is that maybe my coming between you and Simon was the best thing that could have happened to you.'

'Only,' she turned away so that her feelings might be masked, 'you thought little enough of *my* feelings at the time.'

'I admit that. It was Simon I was thinking of. You didn't matter so much. But I *had* been getting Simon out of scrapes for as long as I could remember and I *was* getting a bit fed-up with the task. If I handled it badly, put it down to that. But I still think you had a lucky escape.'

She was in no mood to agree with him. 'I don't suppose it occurs to you that maybe I've longed for marriage and children. It hurts to be told,' her voice broke as she was hit with self-pity, 'that the child you might have had is nearly seven.'

'Yes. And six and four and three.' He said with a return of his early brutal manner. 'Look here, Bianca.' Quite roughly he swung her back to face him, his fingers cutting into the soft skin of her upper arm. 'Simon got married shortly after he went north. A nice girl from Aberdeen and they had four children in as many years. So I still say you're better off as you are. Believe me, he's no great shakes as a husband.'

'Maybe he would have been.' His easy dismissal of Simon made her fiercely defensive. 'If he had been allowed to marry the woman he wanted.'

'No, Bianca.' He smiled and sighed. 'Simon is . . . just Simon. A weak husband might have pleased you for a little while, but by this time you would have been going out of your mind with boredom. Even Morag, and she's nothing like you, even she finds it hard to cope with.'

'Some people don't want as much from life. He's got his job and . . . '

'He didn't last in store management. He left that and went to college to train as a social worker, but he didn't like that either. Now they have a small grocery shop and sub-post office in a country town in Fife.'

'Lots of people see that as an ideal life.' Bianca felt that slowly, surely, she was losing the argument. 'Away from the rat race.'

'Would you, Bianca?' There was a pause before he spoke, a pause which he seemed to use persuasively, his eyes holding hers with a gentle strength, his mouth revealing a faint disarming smile. 'Would you rather be there, serving pounds of butter and second-class stamps, than down here, doing whatever it is that you do?'

'Who's to say?' she burst out in a last desperate attempt. 'Who's to say whether I would rather be there. But at least if I disliked it then I would have myself to blame, I would have had the pleasure of making my own mistakes.'

This time the smile reached his eyes, to her surprise and indignation he put back his head and laughed. She saw the strong white teeth, the long dark throat contrasting with the dazzling lace-frilled shirt front. 'You cannot believe that, Bianca.' As he shook his head at her the smile faded. 'You must know how much more satisfactory it always is when you can blame someone else for whatever goes wrong in life. All these years you have been blaming me.' He put out his hands catching her again by the shoulders, shaking her a little but without rancour. 'I wouldn't mind betting you've enjoyed it. Confess.'

Bianca stared at him, hardly hearing what he was saying, conscious only of the disastrous way she was feeling. Every faint pressure of his fingers was sending throbbing sensations quivering to her nerve endings. It was so disturbing, so bewildering that she couldn't think. He seemed to take her silence for agreement because his expression mellowed even further, and she got the impression of some powerful force pulling them together, although she was sure the distance between them did not alter.

'You know, Bianca.' There was a thoughtful note in his voice as he gazed down at her. 'Bianca, it's a pretty name. How did you get it?'

All her animosity towards him seemed to be melting away. 'My grandmother was Spanish. She was Bianca.'

'And yet you changed it to a thing as ugly as Bee?' He paused and his eyes were warm on her face. 'You've changed, Bianca.' She felt a tremor inside her every time he repeated it and he seemed to be doing it often enough. 'I'm not surprised I didn't know you at first. You've changed from a pretty girl into a beautiful woman. The name is all part of the pattern.'

Then she really did feel she was moving towards him, his head bent closer to hers as if he meant to kiss her and she, idiotically, had her mouth half-raised when, luckily, there was a commotion outside the door and they moved apart.

'Darling.' It was Freddie, reproachful, pouting, gorgeous who burst through, moving swiftly towards Daniel and thrusting a hand through his arm smiled up into his face before she turned her glittering cold eyes on Bianca. 'How could you desert me after bringing me to this party? I thought you said it was business?'

'It was, darling.' While he dropped a kiss on the top of her head his attention seemed focussed on the other girl. 'Bianca and I had something important to discuss.'

'Oh.' A tiny frown marred the perfection of her

features. 'I have the feeling . . .' she began, but before she could say any more Daniel pulled her round to face him with the same confidence he had used to Bianca shortly before.

'And I have the feeling, Freddie, that I would like something to eat.' As he guided his partner to the door he sent a quite blatant message in Bianca's direction. But she, feeling only relief that she had been prevented from making a fool of herself—again—could only feel absurdly grateful that Freddie's interruption had come in time.

For the rest of the evening, Bianca gave Daniel Bohun as wide a berth as she had during the early part of the evening. Only this time she was much less clear in her motives. Then she had been merely feeding the fury which had simmered away fairly quietly for eight years. Years during which all her thought for him had been malevolent. She hadn't quite got round to making little wax effigies and sticking them with pins, but that was how her mind had worked on the whole.

But now, since her talk with him, she found her attitude strangely changed. It wasn't that any of his arguments had convinced her, she was as certain about his interference as she had ever been, but he had forced her to examine a fact that had occurred to her from time to time over the years. Forced her to admit that there was some truth in what he had suggested.

She had been too young all those years ago. And Simon had been too young. The thought of a man, especially a man, tying himself down for life before he had seen anything of life itself was one that now appalled her. It was sad that Simon hadn't heeded his cousin. Having been thwarted once it seemed he had been determined to assert his right to marry whenever he liked. And whoever. There was a faint stab of the familiar pain, but it was very faint. More for Simon and his wife, Morag, Daniel had called her—more for them than for herself.

It was true, compared with Morag she had it made. And deep down a trickle of thankfulness stirred, grateful that some power, some guardian angel had been watching over her, had prevented her from taking the final step. She shivered then whirled round when she heard a voice close to her ear.

'We've come to say goodnight, Bianca.' Daniel Bohun was looking down at her with a strangely intimate expression on his face. At his elbow Lex hovered while half a step away Cindy was trying to hold Freddie's attention—Freddie, who was watching Bianca with a tinge of jealousy and a frown of perplexity.

'Oh . . .' It was impossible to look anywhere but into his eyes. 'Are you going now?'

'Yes.' A faint smile curved the thinnish lips. 'We have a long drive.'

'Well, goodnight.' For no reason that she could think of Bianca felt her colour rise and held out her hand. Immediately she regretted that, because his touch was strange, unbearably sweet, impossibly painful. She removed her fingers as quickly as she could, switching her attention to his companion, regardless now whether the stewardess recognised her or not.

Together they walked to the door and just before they finally said goodbye Freddie asked, still with that frustrated uncertain expression, 'Have you been on any flights recently, Bianca?'

'Come on, darling.' Daniel, who had been deep in conversation with Lex and Cindy, put out a hand and drew her protectively to him. 'Say goodnight and let's go.' And obediently Freddie did just that.

The rest of the weekend was obviously an anti-climax. At least Bianca found it so though she didn't doubt that Cindy was glad that the party was successfully in the past. Lex at least seemed a bit more relaxed although every time the telephone rang he jumped to answer it. Most of the time the calls were from the previous night's guests who had rung to say a few words of thanks and after listening for a few moments Lex inevitably handed the instrument over to his wife.

But when they returned from a long walk on the Saturday afternoon, Cindy and Bianca found Lex looking positively cheerful as he waited for them at the front door. They had just closed it behind them when he spoke to his wife with an expression of satisfaction.

'Daniel phoned.'

'Oh?'

'Yes. Just to thank us for last night, that kind of thing.'

'Excuse me.' Without waiting to hear any more of the conversation, Bianca ran lightly upstairs to her bedroom. She hoped no one had noticed her reaction to the mere mention of his name. Damn, damn, damn! She lay back against the closed door, her eyes lifted upwards as if she were imploring some indulgence from the Almighty. Then she gave herself a mental shake and crossed to the dressing-table.

How silly can you be? She sighed and adopted a self-mocking expression. First of all you spend half the night going over it all, and you end up agreeing with him—although wild horses could hardly drag the admission from you—and then to crown it all, whenever someone mentions his name, you go weak at the knees. You might have to try some aversion therapy, Bianca. Next time one of his programmes is on, you must watch it while having Elspeth beat the soles of your feet with birch twigs.

'It's been nice seeing you, Bianca.' Lex drove her to the station to catch the early train on Monday morning. 'I'm glad we persuaded you against going back last night. Apart from anything else the trains aren't safe for girls to travel on at weekends.'

Bianca was disinclined to argue with her brother-in-law, especially now that the weekend, a more pleasant weekend than usual, was over, so she smiled. 'It was kind of you to ask me. And I was especially glad to have the chance of a long chat with Cindy. I'm thrilled at her news.' She slid a glance at Lex's uncompromising profile. 'If you had waited much longer I'd have been too old to be an auntie.'

'Oh? In that case isn't it time you had some kids of your own? No sign of meeting some chap who wants to marry you?'

'Maybe I'm the one who doesn't want to.' She was piqued by his cool assumption that a woman was just waiting to be asked.

'You know what I mean.' He dismissed her comment. 'Or are all the men blind these days?'

'Not quite.' she said demurely. 'I've decided to settle for a career. Until—' she yawned and stretched, releasing her seatbelt as they turned into the station yard, '—until I meet someone who'll drive all thoughts of career out of my mind. But if I have to wait much longer I'll be giving up hope.'

'I wouldn't if I were you.' Lex reached into the boot for her case. 'Was I wrong in thinking that Daniel Bohun was giving you a kind of special look the other night? And he did say you had met before. Something to do with business, was it?'

'Something like that.' She smiled as she took the case from him. 'Oh, and you are wrong Lex. The only look Daniel Bohun gave me was one of sheer disdain.'

So presumably Lex would have been as surprised as Bianca herself was the following week when Daniel Bohun suddenly appeared in the sumptuous offices of Fantasque U.K. She was busy poring over some plans for a training week involving all the consultants from north Europe when the buzzer connecting her with her secretary in the outer office went at her elbow.

'Yes, Jane?'

'It's the chairman, Miss Hill. He would like to see you in his office at about twelve noon.'

'Oh?' Bianca's confidence was still not proof against such an unexpected summons. Her heart was suddenly hammering against her ribs. 'Did he say exactly what he wanted, Jane?'

'No. Just, "is Miss Hill in the office this morning?" When I said that you had no engagements today he asked me to give you the message.'

'Himself?'

'Himself. So it's got to be something important.'

'Yes. All right, Jane. Thanks.' But ten minutes after she had got the message Bianca put all her graphs and figures back into the folder. Plans for the conference demanded all her attention and now she had lost her concentration. There were other less important things she could do until midday. She picked up a pile of letters from her in-tray and began to deal with them.

At least she would pass muster with Cyrus J. Wilbur she decided as she prepared to go upstairs to meet the chairman. The cream silk suit, its knobbly slub finish resembling wool more than silk, was simple, its plainness relieved by the brilliantly subtle shade of the blouse that went with it. Now green was a colour which she could wear. It looked fabulous with her copper-coloured hair.

Today she wore it in a rather severe chignon controlled by a plain tortoiseshell clasp. In her ears she had studs in the vibrant colour of her blouse, her make-up skilfully understated as it always was during working hours. She stood in the lift that whisked her to the penthouse suite where the chairman had his office and his flat, studying herself with nervous uncertainty which showed in the way her long pink-tipped fingers played with the strands of gold chain about her neck.

But when the doors slid open and she stepped out into the opulent hall, all her nervousness seemed to leave her. What on earth was she afraid of? It had been the chairman's decision which had got her the job, so why should she work herself up into a state thinking he had summoned her to give her a rocket? He had been mildness itself when he had listened to her report when she returned last week from New York. And since then she knew she hadn't committed any awful blunders.

Confidently she walked into the outer office, and raised an enquiring eyebrow at Mary Jennings.

'Go right in, Miss Hill,' his PA smiled. 'The chairman is waiting for you.'

Mr Wilbur lifted his bulk from the chair behind the wide desk and raised a welcoming hand which immediately dispelled any lingering worry about his purpose in bringing her up to his office. 'Ah Bianca, I'm so pleased that you could spare us some of your time.'

Us. It was only when he used the plural that Bianca realised he was not alone in the room. That and the way he waved towards a figure whose long legs could just be seen extending from one of the leather wing armchairs which faced his desk.

Something about the legs sent warning messages to Bianca's brain. Messages which were at once dismissed as being too utterly ridiculous. What possible reason could there be for Dani . . .

'I understand you and Daniel Bohun have already met, Bianca.' It was true. All doubt was removed when the long legs unfolded themselves and she found herself looking into the eyes of the man who had hardly been out of her mind since the weekend. And, she corrected subconsciously, for eight years before that.

He was wearing a dark suit, navy with a tiny over-check, white shirt and what looked like an old school tie. He looked, for him, slightly tense but his serious expression softened as he absorbed her appearance.

'Hello, Bianca.' He waited till she had taken her seat before sitting down again and she felt his eyes on her all the time she concentrated on the chairman, now busy with glasses and a crystal decanter.

'Thank you.' In need of reviving she took the glass offered and sipped at the golden liquid.

'Well, may I be allowed a small toast.' When he was being playful the chairman could be ponderous indeed, Bianca thought sourly as her eyes smiled at him over the rim of her glass. 'Success,' Cyrus J Wilbur raised his glass, 'to your joint venture. You, Bianca. And you, Daniel.' He sat down without appearing to notice Bianca's choking, her attempt to find a handkerchief in the pocket of her jacket, her acceptance of the one that was held out towards her. She mopped up the spilt sherry with the large white handkerchief with the initial D embroidered in white in one corner. Still she refused to look at him and in any case the chairman was talking again.

'You look a bit bewildered, Bianca. So I'd better explain. You know we're launching a big publicity campaign and naturally the springboard for that is television. Just by chance I happened to meet Daniel the other night at a party.' Bianca took advantage of the time the chairman spent in rummaging in his top drawer for a file to glare at Daniel who looked quite the picture of innocence. She must have murmured something, for Mr Wilbur looked up in surprise.

'Did you say something, Bianca?'

'Just,' she returned her attention to her employer, 'that . . . some people get around.'

'Oh.' A puzzled look hung about the chairman's rather knowing face then he smiled. 'I think she means you, Daniel. Right, Bianca?'

'I certainly wasn't criticising you, chairman.'

'I see. I think she's getting at you.' It was all a great joke to him. 'Must be jealous of that pretty blonde you go around with.'

'No.' As she shook her pretty head, Bianca smiled determinedly. 'No.' Still smiling she looked at Daniel who merely put his head to one side, his expression suggesting disappointment.

'Anyway,' the chairman's next statement quite took the rug from beneath Bianca's feet, 'he can put you in the picture over lunch, I'm sure.'

'Lunch?' The breath was suddenly sucked from her body. 'Are we going out to lunch?'

'You,' the chairman nodded. 'And Daniel.'

'Oh, but . . .' The buzzer went before she could advance her quite positive reasons for not having lunch with Daniel Bohun. But she did have time to admit the truth to herself—that she *dare* not allow herself to be taken out to lunch by him. While she vaguely heard the chairman continuing his conversation with his secretary, she turned to Daniel Bohun so that he should be under no misapprehension about the strength of her feelings. But he was the most obtuse man. He merely looked back at her with an eyebrow raised, an expression on his lips which told her that he was having difficulty in controlling his amusement.

She frowned, drained her glass and returned her attention to the chairman. But he apparently was the last person from whom she could expect support. Smiling benignly he waved an arm in the direction of the door.

'Off you go, both of you. I may be kept here for some time. It's to do with our plans for the Middle East. Daniel will explain it all to you, Bianca.'

And somehow, she wasn't certain how it happened, Bianca found herself being led across the upper corridor and into the lift. Daniel Bohun had his fingers on her elbow and though it was silly to imagine it, she felt as if they were burning through the cloth.

The lift doors had silently closed before she was able to put her protest into words that he could not possibly mistake.

'How dare you.' Her voice trembled with histrionic rage. 'How dare you manoeuvre me into this ridiculous situation!'

'Ridiculous?' He frowned. 'I'm sorry, I'm not quite with you yet.'

'How on earth did you concoct some excuse to come along here?' The lift stopped at her floor, and she tapped angrily across the tiled floor to her office with Daniel Bohun beside her. She glared as he bent across to open the door for her then followed her inside, across Jane's

office and into her own. 'And,' she went on as if there
had been no pause in the conversation, 'trap me with this
silly excuse about . . .' She stopped, unable to remember
just what reason the chairman had put forward for his
visit.

'You mean—' without waiting to be invited, he took
the seat opposite the desk then, again without permission, he brought out a gold cigar case, extracted a thin
cigar and lit it. 'You mean,' he held it for a moment
between strong white teeth then blew the smoke from
him, 'you consider the whole publicity project both silly
and ridiculous?'

'Of course not. You know exactly what I mean. It's a
strange coincidence that I should meet you three times in
one week. More than coincidence I should have
thought.'

'But then,' some deep secret amusement brought a
sparkle to his eyes. 'you did go out of your way, on that
first occasion, to make an impression on me.' The long
lashes dropped, hiding his expression.

Unexpectedly, Bianca felt an impulse to respond but
she quashed it at once. It would be dangerous to relax
with this man.

'But in any case you're wrong. My coming here today
was planned weeks ago. Before I knew,' his eyes flicked
open to confuse her again, 'there was such a person as
Bianca Hill.'

'Oh . . .' Her assurance floundered. Was it possible to
believe such a thing?

'But,' he pressed on before she could question him
about that, 'we'd better get along. I ordered a table for
one and I don't want to be late.' He uncurled his length
from her chair and walked to the window. 'Do you have
a coat?'

'No.' Bianca grew more flustered. 'But I'll just get a scarf.'

She spent a few minutes in her small private cloakroom looking at herself in the mirror, her expression a mixture of excitement and annoyance. How dared he trap her into this farcical situation? How dared she be such a fool as to *think* of refusing!

When she emerged he swung round from the window, noticing every detail of her appearance, from the top of her glossy head to the high-heeled brown sandals.

'You know, Bianca,' he took a step towards her, stood for a moment frowning down at her, 'the more I see of this,' his eyes left hers to skim approvingly round the comfortable office with all the paraphernalia which added to her senior executive status, 'the more convinced I am that I was right.'

'I've a feeling,' she was rather pleased that he had offered such an opening, 'that you will often find yourself in that situation.' She led the way to the door so that he should be denied her smile.

They were in the lift on their way to the ground floor before he spoke again, then it was with some wholly matter-of-fact enquiry about the presentation of Fantasque in some commercials.

'I'm . . . I'm not certain.' Certainly she had been unprepared to be quizzed on a subject she knew little about.

But he went on with a probing flow of questions so that by the time they settled into the rear seat of a taxi she was feeling angry with herself for giving such an inadequate performance, but even more angry with him for being the cause and witness of her incompetence.

'So you see, Bianca,' he sat in the opposite corner of the seat and surveyed her critically, 'it's all perfectly genuine. Not just a silly excuse as you implied.'

She looked back at him resentfully, wishing with all her heart she could afford to stop the taxi and tell him to go to hell. But even as she stared she saw his lips twitch, and his eyes began to sparkle as he sat forward in the seat, took her chin in his fingers and shook his head as if he too were wondering what was happening.

'Yes, it's perfectly true, Bianca. And if it hadn't been, then I should just have had to think of something else, shouldn't I?' But before she could even begin to understand his cryptic remark the taxi had stopped, and he was holding her hand as he helped her out on to the street.

CHAPTER FOUR

It was a perfectly ordinary lunch. At least it was perfect and on the other hand it was ordinary. The food was good, as good as she had come to expect in some of the small tucked-away restaurants in London. And this one, entered by an inconspicuous door in a Chelsea back street, was transformed the moment you crossed the threshold into an extremely elegant eating place.

She followed the head waiter who greeted her escort by name before he led them towards a table set in a window corner and overlooking a central garden.

'This is pleasant.' Bianca smiled at him across the white linen cloth.

'Isn't it.' But somehow she got the impression he was not meaning the room they had just entered and her mind flicked back to that incomprehensible remark in the taxi. To hide her blush she raised the large handwritten menu and it was not lowered until she had thoroughly noted her favourite dishes and come to a decision.

'Well?' His raised eyebrow suggested he was all too aware of her feelings. 'Have you made up your mind?'

'I'll have whitebait and *boeuf en croûte,* if I may.'

'Mmm. A wise choice.' He frowned over his own choice and went on with an air of abstraction. 'And you may . . . have anything you like.' He looked up at the hovering waiter. 'Two whitebait, one *boeuf en croûte* and I'll have a roast sirloin. And a selection of vegetables. Oh, and a bottle of Grand-Pontet.'

It was a relief, perhaps just a little bit disappointing, too, when he guided the conversation along business lines. But when she had finished the main course, Bianca discovered that she was being drawn out, very gently and discreetly, about her life after their first traumatic meeting.

'And then,' she concluded, cradling her glass in her hands and looking deeply into the dark red wine, 'when we were taken over by Fantasque I was offered my present job. It was a bit of a relief because we didn't know what was going to happen to us. We thought we might disappear without trace. You know all the stories you read in the papers about take-overs, especially concerning American firms.'

'Mmm. And you're obviously loving the job. You look to me as if you were made for it—or it for you.' He frowned. 'I hope that you and Cyrus J Wilbur are not . . .'

'No, we're not.' She laughed, slightly surprised that she could take his teasing so lightly. 'Not with Mrs Cyrus J living upstairs and keeping such a firm eye on him.'

'So, that's all that's keeping you back.' He leaned back, one hand stretched out to touch the stem of his glass.

'That's all.' Dramatically she put her fingers to the firm curve of her breast, but withdrew it swiftly when she saw his eyes follow the gesture. 'I hoped no one would guess I was madly in love with him.' Colour stained her cheeks; her eyes, disturbed by the expression in his, looked away.

'I hadn't guessed. So it's all right. Now,' seeming to take pity on her, he gestured to the waiter who came towards them holding out the menus. 'What kind of pudding will you have?'

'I couldn't eat any more. Really.'

'You must,' he sounded abstracted, 'otherwise I

shan't be able to have one. And I hate to be thwarted.'

'How like a man.'

'Yes, we're all alike.' He glanced at the waiter. 'One vacherin, one apple pie with cheese.' As he faced Bianca, he leaned his arms on the table. 'When they come you can choose which you'll have. I don't mind.'

'I'll be putting on pounds.' She slid a slender finger beneath the band of her skirt. 'Then it's such a struggle to get it off again.'

'You won't. Not just this once. For this is a special occasion, don't forget.'

'A special occasion?' From force of habit her eyes flirted with him over her glass.

'Yes, you and I are supposed to be making some arrangements about this television promotion.'

'Oh?' Would her disappointment show?

'And besides, it's to celebrate the peace that has blossomed between us.' He looked up as the waiter arrived and stood indecisively with the plates until Bianca gestured that the apple pie should be put in front of her companion. 'Hasn't it, Bianca?' He paused with a forkful of tart poised between plate and mouth.

'I suppose so.' The long dark lashes shielded her from his scrutiny. 'But it's a pity you're still getting *everything* your own way.'

'Am I? I didn't realise.'

Bianca burst out laughing, and looked up into his face disbelievingly. 'Of course you did. You never intended I should have the apple pie. Ordering the cheese with it was just your subtle way of telling me it was yours. Admit it.'

'My story is that I chose the vacherin specially with you in mind. I did think you would prefer that.'

'Oh, and suppose—' intently Bianca chased the last

piece of meringue round the plate, '—suppose I told you
I have a passion for apple pie?'

'In that case I'll order apple pie for you next time.'

In that moment, Bianca looked up, caught the expression on his face and was robbed of the smart retort
she would have liked to make. So there's going to be a
next time? She didn't need to ask it. The answer was in
his face for anyone to see. And he was the kind of man
who always got his own way. He had made that perfectly
plain. She felt a strange escalation in the excitement she
had been aware of since twelve noon that day. And now
it was . . . somewhere in the region of three o'clock. A
kind of hopeless, carefree joy took hold of her which two
cups of strong black coffee did nothing to subdue.

Even when she was safely back in her office with the
door closed and Daniel Bohun gone about his business,
whatever that was, she could not bring her thoughts back
down to earth. She knew she was behaving crazily, in a
way that a week earlier she would have thought impossible, but . . .

The plans for the training conference were making
even less sense than they had done before and with a
groan of despair she pushed them away from her.
Tomorrow she really would have to make an effort to get
on top of the project. And yet . . . She sighed. How could
she when she simply had to have her hair done? And
when she knew that in the evening she would be going
out with him?

Not that she had agreed to such a thing. He hadn't
even troubled to ask her, simply he had made the
statement that he would call for her, that they would
drive along the river to a thirties-style roadhouse where
they could dine and dance. And she had felt herself
smiling submissively, as if she were in the habit of doing

just what she was told! In fact, the sole attraction might be the sheer novelty of having the decisions made for her. It wouldn't last, of course. But she would allow herself to enjoy it for just a little while.

But next evening she was as excited as a girl on her first date. More so, in fact; she could never remember this trembling, verging on ecstatic feeling when she had been young. Not even with Simon had she felt just as quivery as this. Elspeth, coming into the bedroom where she was getting ready, told her as much with the frankness of familiarity.

'Well,' she leaned against the door upright, 'you surprise me, going to such trouble over a man you don't even like.'

'Trouble? I haven't gone to that much trouble,' Bianca lied without a blush. 'But in my position I can't afford to be seen looking less than well-made-up. You know that.' She frowned as she flicked a little gold on the ends of her long thick lashes.

'Well, you can make what excuses you like, but I'm sure it's not just so you can publicise Fantasque that you're going to such limits.' She came forward into the room. 'I still can't understand it. How is it you have him eating out of your hand just days after you made him look so foolish in that picture? What did your sister think of it?'

'Oh, Cindy didn't know. Thank goodness.' Bianca stood back to check her appearance, decided that the camisole-top dress in a brown silky material would be just right for the thirties scene, as she could take off the little jacket if they should decide to dance. At the thought her hand paused in the act of doing her lips and her almond-shaped eyes returned her look of dismay. Dance . . . With Daniel Bohun . . .? Oh no . . . Oh . . .!

'What's wrong, love? Don't say you've changed your

mind. But maybe,' she affected breathless excitement, 'if you say you can't go then he'll take me.'

With an effort Bianca laughed, chasing the goose firmly off her grave. 'You know you won't go out with anyone except Jim.'

'Well, I'm not so sure. I might be like you, unable to resist the man if he should glance in my direction.'

'It doesn't mean that I can't resist him,' Bianca stretched her mouth to take another smear of colour, 'just because I'm going out with him.'

'Mmm. I'm not going to be so easy to convince. There's an entirely different look about you since the weekend with your sister. After all, you've had plenty of boy-friends and so I'm in a position to judge. I bet you you'll be married to Daniel Bohun before the end of t e year.'

Bianca laughed. 'Now I know you're potty.' But further conversation was interrupted by the doorbell.

'How long have you shared with Elspeth?' They were cocooned together in the warmth of his car, the radio dispensed music, sweet and emotional rather than romantic, making Bianca even more aware of everything than she had ever been before.

'Oh, two years. But I've known her for much longer. She used to share with her cousin, then when Myra went abroad to work, she asked me if I'd like to move in with her. It suits both of us and we get on well together. Only . . .'

'Only . . .?' he prompted as he glanced momentarily at her in the half dark.

'Only,' Bianca spoke with reluctance not wishing to bring up the subject, 'Elspeth will be getting married soon and going to live in Northampton. She's engaged to a doctor. At the moment he's on a round-the-world yacht trip, but they'll be marrying the moment he gets back.

'Pity she didn't go with him. Sounds like a perfect honeymoon.'

'Sounds like hard work to me,' Bianca replied sharply, then relenting, 'in any case she suffers from seasickness.'

'Ah well,' he teased, 'that would probably spoil things.' There was a moment's silence while he swung the long sleek car on to a minor road. 'And what will you do then? Look for someone else to live in the flat?'

'No, I don't think so. I don't know anyone well enough to want to share with them. And besides, now that I'm a highly paid executive,' her laugh mocked her pretensions, 'I can afford the rent myself. Actually it will be rather nice to have the extra space. Sometimes we have people coming to the company on business, especially from the States, and I would quite like it if I could offer to put them up for a night or two, and so repay some of the hospitality I had when I was out there.'

They drove into the car park of the roadhouse before any more could be said and moments later they were being shown to one of the tables set around the mellow wood floor.

'Oh, Daniel,' she spoke without thinking, her eyes shining with enthusiasm as they looked about the room, taking in each detail of the art nouveau decor, oblivious of his unwinking contemplation of her vivid features. 'It's nice. And a real live orchestra.' Her eyes moved to the huge uncurtained windows and beyond to where the lights were reflected on the waters of the Thames flowing smoothly past. 'It's almost like being on board ship; in the dining-room, waiting for the band to strike up.' Her voice trailed away at the end when she became aware of his lack of response as well as the unexpected look in his eyes. 'Wh-what have I said?' Colour flooded into her cheeks. 'Am I chattering too much?'

Before he spoke his hand reached across the table, his fingers closed over hers and he totally ignored everything she had said. 'Do you know,' his dark eyes seemed fixed on her mouth causing her emotions, already taut and quivering from the touch of his hand, to tremble still further, 'that is the first time you have used my name.' A thumb moved sensuously against her palm.

'Oh?' Her mind was too blank to make any sensible comment.

'Does that mean, Bianca,' and now there was a suggestion of laughter in his voice, 'that you were simply off guard? Or dare I hope that you have forgiven me. Finally.'

She couldn't imagine what her reply might have been if the orchestra hadn't chosen that precise moment to begin, with the low seductive sound of clarinets playing some tune which Bianca knew but couldn't put a name to. Around them chairs were pushed back as couples went on to the floor and began to move in time to the music, and when he smiled across and asked if she would like to dance, she did not trouble to hide her willingness.

Although she wasn't very expert at this kind of dancing, he made it easy by holding her close so that they moved in unison. But those feelings of bewilderment which had affected her so strongly back at the table were not likely to be dispelled by this situation. Circling the floor to the strains of sweet music, her body closely held against his she was vibrantly aware of each beat of her heart against his chest. If he should be aware of it too! She risked a swift upward glance but that only led to a close encounter with his cheek, an encounter from which neither of them seemed inclined to withdraw.

She tried deliberately to distract herself by an attempt to identify the cologne he used but in the end she failed. Either on him it smelled different, slightly spicy yet astringent with just a touch of the Orient, or it was one that was entirely new to her. His skin was firm and smooth against hers and as if cunningly aware of her thoughts he moved his cheek very slightly making her feel the rasp, very gentle but very male, of his closely-shaven face.

The music stopped and, fingers entwined, they went back to their table where a few moments were spent in discussing the menu with the waiter. It was only then that he leaned forward, captured her fingers again and demanded an answer to his earlier question. 'Which is it, Bianca?'

First she shook her head a little as if by denying certain facts she could dismiss them. But even as she did so, feeling her hair moving cloudily about her bare shoulders, seeing his eyes flick for a split second from her face to its drift, her senses confirmed what her heart was telling her.

'Yes.' She gave a little shrug, at the same time revealing a tiny weak feminine smile of submission.

'Yes?' he insisted. 'Do you mean you were off guard?' The confidence in the way he took her hand closer to him dispelled the notion that he had any belief in that. 'Or that the past . . . is forgotten?'

'You know which.' Suddenly shy, she looked down at the cloth. 'Must I say it?'

'No.' The look in his eyes was fathomless. 'No, you need not.' And he pressed a kiss on to the palm of her hand. 'At least, not this moment.'

As Bianca received the intimate caress she admitted to herself that she was blissfully happy. But one tiny corner at the back of her mind told her to be careful, advised her to remember that this man, the one who was sitting opposite, who was smiling so distractingly into her eyes, who held her with such tenderness when they danced, was the very same man who had been the cause of such anguish eight years ago. But another part of her mind more surely was telling her that eight years ago he had saved her from ruining her life and now . . . But the future was too dazzling to contemplate, she would not risk disappointment by trying to look into it. Live for the moment would be her motto. At least for tonight.

It was late when they left to drive home to London and Bianca snuggled down comfortably in the seat, loving the way he wrapped a mohair rug about her shoulders as if she were something precious, something to be spoiled.

When they stopped in front of the block of flats where Bianca lived everything was still, there was no traffic in the street, no lights shining from any of the windows. Hand in hand they climbed the flight of stairs and when they entered the flat he stood silently watching while she poured boiling water on the instant coffee.

It was difficult for her to pretend to concentrate on the task while all the time she was so aware of the dark figure lounging against the door. Then just before she picked up the cups to lead the way into the sitting-room, she felt his hand on her arm and he was turning her towards him with an impatience that found an immediate echo deep within her.

At first his lips were cool as if detachment were his usual approach, then his mouth seemed to burn against hers, and she was folded closer to the curve of his body as if they were both intent on merging. And all the time her mind and physical being were tormented by the explosion of feelings which overwhelmed her.

'Bianca,' he groaned as his mouth at last left hers, and he buried his face in her hair, his hands twisted in the soft tresses. 'Bianca, Bianca, darling.' There was a protest in his voice.

But she felt the thrill of power as the endearment came from his lips. Power that she could evoke such feelings, that her own response should be as overwhelming. Delicately his mouth moved against her cheek, a trail of dropped kisses led to her eyes till her searching mouth found his again.

'Bianca.' When at last he separated from her it was with a tiny groan of protest. Strong hands clasped her shoulders as he held her away and he surveyed her closely, seriously, with an expression that made her hold her breath.

'Let's forget the coffee, shall we?' His voice was slightly husky.

For an instant she misunderstood his meaning, her mind trying to grapple with the totally unexpected speed with which things were developing, and her heart missed a beat. Several beats.

Before she had time to reply she saw his lips move again, heard with a pang of dismay, with disappointment so sharp that it amounted to anguish, words which told her she had jumped to the wrong conclusion.

'I'm afraid coffee would be too much of an anti-climax.' He kissed her, this time a light, controlled pressure of his mouth against her forehead. 'Goodnight, Bianca.'

And the door closed softly behind him before she had time to make a reply. As if she were in a dream, she turned and emptied two cups of tepid coffee down the sink.

Bed was a frustrating anti-climax. From that moment's exposure when she had imagined that he was inviting himself to join her there, to the tormenting reality of her usual unsullied chastity, was quite a jump, so Bianca thought as she lay sleepless in her narrow bed, her mind a confusion of exhilaration and of disappointed hopes. He hadn't even mentioned meeting her again.

The sudden fear that struck at her made her gasp and clutch a pillow soothingly against her. Surely, surely, this wasn't for him one of his casual encounters? There had been something more to it, for him as much as for her, she was certain. Only—Pain waxed. She wasn't really the world's most brilliant judge of character, was she?

Another thought came to torment her, one that she had cast conveniently aside in the last few days. Freddie. Freddie Galston. The girl he took around with him when he went to parties. The girl he was in all likelihood having an affair with. He might even be living with her, but in her job she would be away a great deal and he would want a few spares to fill in the lonely evenings during those spells. Tonight could have been such an occasion.

Bianca gave a little sob and pressed her face into the pillow. She mustn't think a single date meant anything. Daniel Bohun had probably had more dates in the last six months than she had had in the whole of her life. If she *did* hear from him again, then she must be casual, avoid giving the impression that she had been hanging round the telephone. And just to be on the safe side she had better think of a previous arrangement simply to underline the fact that he was not the only pebble on the beach.

'Bianca.' She recognised the voice immediately, no one else had quite the same deep rich tones, so she was particularly pleased that she heard not the vestige of a tremor in her own reply.

'Daniel, how are you?'

'I'm fine. And you?'

'Yes. Busy of course.'

'Am I disturbing you?' The amusement in his voice told her that he would not believe her even if she said he was.

'Of course not.' That sounded too keen. 'Not really.'

'I tried to ring you from Holland.'

'Holland?' Happiness bubbled inside her like an effervescence. 'I didn't know you were going there.'

'I didn't either. Not till I got a message the day after I saw you. I had to rush off to catch a plane, and there wasn't time to ring and let you know.'

'Oh? Warmth and pleasure suffused her body. 'There was no need to think . . .' He had wanted to ring her . . .

'Of course there was,' he contradicted. 'And I'll be disappointed if you say you didn't expect to hear from me, Bianca.' His voice reminded her that he expected an answer.

'Yes.' Total capitulation. 'I hoped you would ring.'

'Bless you.' Silence throbbed for a moment along the telephone lines. 'Now I want to ask you something.'

'Yes.' She was breathless but tried to sound cagey.

'On Friday night I'm going down to Worcester for the weekend. I was wondering if you would like to come with me.'

'Worcester.' It seemed a moment for a little bit of procrastination while she caught her breath again.

'Yes.' It was a dry amused voice now. 'You have heard of it, I suppose? North of Gloucester and sandwiched between Warwick and Hereford, not too far from the Welsh border.'

'I do know,' she said in what she hoped was a cutting voice, ignoring the fact that geography had always been one of her weaker subjects. It's just that I'm not in the habit of going off for the weekend with men. Especially men whom I hardly know. Especially, she reminded herself as she felt all her inclinations yearn towards Worcester and the Welsh borders, men who have been brutally cruel to me in the past.

'Well.' At that moment Daniel Bohun seemed as unsure of himself as she was. There was a carefully casual manner about him which suggested her reply meant a great deal and that he was just a tiny bit anxious. 'What do you say, Bianca? I plan to leave town about five-thirty. I can pick you up either at the office or at your flat, whichever you like. And we should be there in time for the evening meal.'

Suddenly Bianca made up her mind. All her senses were urging her to go. Even the sound of his voice on the phone was enough to make her heart hammer in a way that was all too unfamiliar, and her fingers were clammy on the receiver as she changed from one hand to the other. It was something which had loomed on to the horizon once or twice in the years since Simon. On these occasions she hadn't been even slightly tempted although she had coolly, calmly assessed whether she ought to take the plunge. After all, she was the only one of her friends, Elspeth excluded, who still clung to such out-of-date moral codes. And she wasn't even certain about Elspeth. She had come back from waving goodbye to Jim with a distinctly dewy look in her eye, a knowledge that hadn't been suddenly revealed to her at her work in the medical practice. So it seemed as if she, Bianca, was the only one left and it was time to change all that. Besides, with every fibre, every nerve in her body, she was longing for him. The last two days had been a nightmare. All she wanted was to be with Daniel, to know that he wanted her, too.

'All right.' She sounded quite matter-of-fact as if she had given the same reply many times to similar invitations.

'Bless you, darling.' The darling caused a throb of something like pain to pulse through her body and at the same time she realised that she had better put Daniel firmly into the picture. Maybe when he discovered the truth he would want to back out. Twenty-five, nearly twenty-six-year-old virgins might not be his idea of a good relaxing weekend.

"Oh, and Daniel—' Now reaction or nerves were setting in, making her voice all trembly and gauche so that she knew she couldn't explain, not like this, not on the telephone. 'What kind of clothes shall I take for the weekend?' It was the only thing she could think of.

'Oh, nothing too fancy. I don't suppose we'll be doing anything very exotic.' What does that mean? she asked herself. A whole weekend spent in bed? 'But whatever you wear you look marvellous. And I know my mother's going to adore you. Goodbye, darling.'

'Goodbye, Daniel.' Bianca admired the restraint which allowed her to reply in a civilised way, although her fingers were too weak to prevent the receiver dropping from her hand on to the cradle.

So, she thought numbly, she was wrong. That *that* kind of weekend was not what he had had in mind. It was just that he intended taking her home to meet his mother. It was some time before the significance of such an invitation percolated through her shattered emotions.

CHAPTER FIVE

WHEN they left on their journey she was still in a state of shock, although it had subsided just a little. Daniel greeted her at the flat with a brief pressure of his cheek against hers and a grin for Elspeth who appeared in the sitting-room doorway at the same moment.

'You don't mind me stealing her for the weekend, do you, Elspeth?'

'Of course not. And it looks as if it's going to be a bit sunny for you. The weather outlook is good.'

'Mmm.' Daniel picked up the suitcase prominently waiting in the middle of the floor. 'Well, see you on Sunday night, Elspeth.'

'Will you want a meal?' Elspeth followed them to the door.

'No, I tell you what, if we're back in time I'll take you both out. Think of a nice place where we can go, Elspeth. Ready, love?' His dark eyes appraised the soft green wool jeans and waistcoat worn over a rust-coloured blouse, and he helped as she struggled to slide her arms into the fawn suede jacket.

Soon they were driving along the motorway, the roof of the sleek coupé pushed back so that they could enjoy the warm air of the late Indian summer. Bianca slid round in her seat so that she could have the wholly satisfying experience of looking at him.

He was wearing navy flannel trousers with a navy-and-white speckled tweed jacket over a scarlet roll-neck sweater; the outfit emphasising width of shoulder and length of leg. But it was his face that held her attention for the longest time; the firm profile concentrating on the road ahead of him. She had not realised just how long his eyelashes were: they curved over his cheeks when he blinked, described tiny arcs beneath strongly marked eyebrows when open.

But she was confused when he flashed a swift grin in her direction, telling her instantly, indirectly that he had been aware of her scrutiny, but that he didn't mind. His message in some peculiar, totally incomprehensible way sent her feelings into a spin from which she recovered only when she realised that he was pulling off the road, into a nearly deserted lay-by.

'What's the matter?' This time her glance was enquiring.

'Nothing.' He pulled on the brake and turned to her, looking intently as he scrutinised each feature, finally smiling down into her eyes. 'Nothing,' he said again as he allowed one finger to trickle seductively along her jawline stopping only when it reached the corner of her mouth, 'except that I've been longing to do this ever since I picked you up. And I knew,' his voice was so soft that she had to incline her head to catch what he said, 'that I could not wait until we got to Worcester . . .'

His mouth on hers, at first delicately teasing, then more demanding, more searching, caused all those awkward feelings, the ones she had been trying to subdue and control, to explode in her bloodstream with instant devastation. She reached her arms about his neck, exulting in the power that strained her body against his, feeling the passion of his responses beating in hectic unison with her own. Awkward feelings? Blissful, exquisite, enchanting feelings. So that even when the long kiss ended, when his arms slackened and slid reluctantly from her waist, she was still suspended half-way between heaven and paradise.

'Darling.' His mouth was still close to hers, and she could feel the warmth of his breath against her cheek, stirring her hair a little as he held her for a moment longer, then put her firmly aside with a smile and gave his attention to the long drive.

Once or twice he searched for her hand, took her fingers to his lips while he drove along, and spoke most of the time of things about which she was curious to know. Details about his mother, for instance, because although she had heard the name Madeleine Bohun, vaguely she had thought that it was Boon and so had never associated the famous avant-garde sculptress with the man she had sworn to hate. Daniel darted a slightly sardonic glance in her direction when she said as much.

'I thought you might have seen her on *Bias*.'

'No, I didn't.' There was a momentary return of her old animosity, but it disappeared too quickly for her to feel more than a brief ache. 'I'm afraid your programmes are too highbrow for me.'

'Highbrow!' he jeered softly. 'You know your only objection to them was the moderator.'

'Don't let's discuss that now.' She averted her eyes firmly from him, staring out at the darkened country-side. 'Otherwise we might not be on speaking terms by the time we reach your mother's house.'

'Well,' he spoke mildly now, 'I'm hoping that when the new series begins you'll be able to bring yourself to look at it.'

'I might.' She was too interested in him and what he was saying to be able to maintain her pretence of detach-ment. 'But I thought you were planning to be more involved in behind-the-scenes work, less with actual programmes.'

'I am. In fact, I'm wondering if this should be the last series. It's had a good run and besides I'd like to find time to do some writing—I just allowed myself to be diverted. You'd be surprised how much research is required even for short programmes on television.'

'Yes, I suppose so.' Aware that they were leaving the main road she swung round to look through the windscreen. 'Oh, and you know that discussion we had about our advertisements, I . . .'

'Oh, darling.' This was one of the times when he reached for her hand and squeezed it gently. 'I thought you knew, I don't really deal with that kind of thing. That was simply a ploy to get into contact with you. I'll put you on to Crispin Daiches, he's the advertising specialist.'

'I see.' Although she spoke coolly, Bianca could not hide the sparkle of pleasure in her eyes which were illuminated by an approaching vehicle. 'I did not realise you could be so devious.'

There was a moment's silence during which he required both hands for steering, then when he spoke again his voice had altered subtly—she was aware of it without being able to identify the change. 'But I can be.' He laughed, a short bitter sound. 'When I want to be, I can be exceedingly devious.'

Bianca did not reply but stared in the darkness, all she could see was the strong profile of a man she had hated and who now seemed to be holding her life, along with all her hopes and dreams, in the palm of his hand. Without understanding why, she shivered slightly, then as she turned away from him he spoke again in his former tone so that she wondered if she had imagined that brief, slightly sinister transformation.

'By the way, have you heard anything from your sister?'

'Cindy?' Bianca's voice showed her surprise. 'Yes, she rang the other night.' And when he did not comment she continued, 'Why do you ask?'

'Just that I've seen your brother-in-law once or twice.'

'Oh.' Bianca paused. 'But I thought you were in Holland.'

'I saw him the day I left and again this morning. Very briefly.'

'I see.' All kinds of troubled thoughts chased themselves round in her mind, worries which she would not unload on Daniel. Not yet at least. 'How was he?'

'He seemed well.' Was it Bianca's imagination that he sounded a bit cagey?

'Have you known him a long time?' she asked.

'A fair number of years. In fact, his first wife was a friend of the family.'

'How cosy.' Bianca couldn't think why she had said something so stupid, but she was relieved that he seemed unwilling to make much of it then.

'Not really. And you needn't feel defensive about your sister. I do understand that divorces happen. After all, my own parents were divorced long before my father died. It's rarely one partner's fault. As far as Lex and Jenni were concerned I think they simply grew apart. He was living and working in London while she was in Taunton where the boys were at school. She liked the country life and Lex hated it, as you might imagine. I dare say both of them are happier now than when they were married.'

'Maybe.' She had forgotten her irritation of a moment before. 'Only I'm not so sure about Cindy. Lex isn't too keen on having a second family which is a bit unfair. Surely he ought to realise that most women want to have children and . . .'

'I think that when men decide to marry,' he grinned in her direction, 'they have other things on their minds, not unconnected with babies, I admit, but few of them are actually worrying about that.'

'Oh.' Bianca was glad that the darkness hid the colour in her cheeks. 'Still, I think that Lex should have realised . . .'

'Maybe Cindy ought to have asked. After all, it seems likely that once a man has reached a certain age, then maybe he's past the time when he wants to be coping with bottles and nappies.'

'Always the man's point of view!' But in spite of herself she could not suppress the giggle that came bubbling from her throat and in response to his glance of enquiry she explained, 'I was just trying to imagine Lex putting on a nappy. And failing.'

'I see what you mean.' Daniel reduced the speed of the car, stretched an arm along the back of her seat so that his hand relaxed intimately against her shoulder, the fingers stroking through the thin silk of her blouse. 'It does take a bit of imagination. But I don't think we should give him up. Think of Charlie Chaplin.'

'If you insist. But I can't say that makes it any easier.' Her laughter faded as Daniel turned into a wide gateway and drove slowly along a gravel drive at the end of which she could see a blaze of lights coming from a rather sprawling house. 'Is this it?' She was all at once aware of her own inadequacies.

'Yes, this is it. And don't worry.' It was strange how

he had seemed to sense her lack of confidence. 'Above all, don't let Maddy overwhelm you.'

'Maddy?' Enormous eyes turned to look enquiringly at him.

'My mother,' he said drily. 'You've come to a very unconventional household, my sweet. I hope it doesn't put you off.'

Unconventional was one way of putting it, Bianca decided, as she looked round the cluttered sitting-room then back at her hostess. But somehow she thought that she and Daniel's mother would get on rather well. To begin with she was much younger than Bianca had imagined—she did a rapid calculation, adding the requisite number to Daniel's thirty-four and coming up with fifty-one or two at the very least.

'You know,' she had a musical voice, and the grand piano on a sort of dais at one end of the room suggested to Bianca that her voice might even have been trained, 'I am so pleased you came down this weekend, darling.' She addressed her son's back while he fixed drinks for them. 'Otherwise, I should have had to call you. Thank you, Daniel.' The hand she put out to take the cut crystal tumbler was well-shaped but workmanlike. She sipped then sighed with satisfaction as if she had had a tiring day and had been waiting for something to stimulate her. 'Next week I'm off to the States.'

'Are you?' He didn't seem surprised but threw himself down into one of the large chintz-covered seats. 'This thing in Kent come off?' He raised a dark eyebrow.

'Mmm. That's it. It's come up a bit earlier than I thought.' She turned her dark eyes, so like her son's, towards Bianca, smiling at her and pushing back the long dark hair from her face. 'Have you been to the States, Bianca?'

'Yes.' Recollection of just how that trip had ended brought the colour to the girl's face and Daniel's raised mocking eyebrow, glimpsed from the corner of her eye, did nothing to relieve her confusion. 'Yes, I was there quite recently for the first time.'

'How exciting.' She sighed nostalgically. 'I'll never forget my first trip there.'

'When was that, Mrs Bohun?' She asked the question formally, still aware of Daniel's amusement, refusing to look at him.

'Oh, please. Not Mrs Bohun. Make it Madeleine. Formality makes me feel as if I have one foot in the grave, and I'm not as old as I look!' The remark invited a compliment but she hurried on before one could be delivered. 'I was a mere child when Daniel was born. When I went to register his birth I was told my mother would have to come herself.' She laughed, showing small white teeth, then got to her feet. 'Now I must go and see how things are getting on in the kitchen. Pierre gets temperamental if I leave him too long. Take Bianca up to her room, darling. There's masses of hot water if you want baths and I'll see you both at dinner in about half an hour.'

As she followed Daniel up the narrow winding staircase, Bianca lowered her head obediently to avoid a low beam then gasped when on the landing he suddenly caught her by the shoulders.

'You're laughing.' His own eyes sparkled with amusement so that she felt it safe to allow hers to express itself.

'Oh Daniel, isn't she wonderful!'

'She's wonderful,' he agreed, 'so long as you don't have to live with her. The times—' he groaned comically as he released her, took up Bianca's case again and led her along a short corridor which parted from the main landing, '—the times at school when I longed to have an ordinary, conventional mother. The kind who arrived in a Morris Traveller with a cocker spaniel in the back, dressed in tweeds—the mother not the spaniel!—or a plain dress, nothing way out. The frantic prayers the night before Parents' Day.' He laughed. 'The times I was disappointed.'

Bianca's heart melted in sympathy. 'Poor Daniel. Was it very awful?'

'Very,' he assured her as he paused with his fingers on a door handle, 'but in the end always great fun. Once she arrived in a huge open car, a Corniche, and she packed it with boys—the ones whose parents lived abroad and couldn't be there—and took us to the seaside for the day. We stuffed ourselves with candy floss and ice-cream then she took us all to tea at the Grand Hotel. I remember the head waiter looking down his nose at this mob of untidy schoolboys with the mad woman, but he let us in. Probably thought she was some kind of eccentric noblewoman. She adopted that haughty manner which had us all in stitches while she dispensed the tea. Then when we were back in the dormitory that night, all the boys who had come with us told the tale of our outrageous day. After that I went to public school and I didn't seem to mind so much, I suppose I was getting older and of course the boys, some of them were eighteen or nineteen, they couldn't keep their eyes off Mama.' He grinned. 'It has its compensations you know, having a mother like that.' He turned the handle and stood back so that she could go into the room ahead of him and flicked the light switch.

'Daniel, what a lovely room.' And it was, although quite different from what the slightly chaotic downstairs had led her to expect. There was a sloping ceiling and the walls were covered with a cottagey paper strewn with mauve flowers and green ivy. Matching curtains hung at the deep-set windows and the cover on the single bed was quilted in the same material. On the floor was a carpet in a deeper mauve, a thick velvet pile over which her feet moved soundlessly and in which she would enjoy curling her bare toes.

There was a small dressing-table in one corner, a green velvet-covered chair in another and behind one of the doors would surely be an old-fashioned cupboard.

'It's all right, is it?' Daniel asked in a businesslike tone as he deposited her case on the stool at the end of the bed. 'Bathroom's through here.' And he opened what she had taken for the cupboard door. 'It's a tiny bath, I'm afraid; it was all they could fit in when the re-did the place.'

'It's more than all right.' She poked her head inside the door, liking the look of the deep bath in white porcelain, exactly right in a house like this. 'I love it.'

'Well, it wasn't always like this. When Maddy took over the three tumble-down cottages we all thought she was mad, but it's come all right in the end. There's a large building at the bottom of the garden, an old barn which she uses as a studio. For a long time she worked in the sitting-room, but in the end Pierre eased her out of the house and now even forbids her to set foot in any of the spare bedrooms. Says she just has to look at a room to create chaos. Oh, and by the way,' about to leave her he paused and looked at her with a quizzical expression, 'Pierre came several years ago ostensibly to help her with the restoration, then stayed on as a kind of house-man. Now he's cook-housekeeper and general facto-tum. You'll meet him at dinner for he lives *'en famille'*. What their real relationship is I don't know and I don't

take the trouble to find out. But they get along well
enough together and as far as I'm concerned that's all
that matters.'

Bianca stared at the door which closed behind him,
then after a few seconds she moved slowly to a chair and
sat down. When he had been speaking of his mother and
Pierre, Daniel had been a little bit on the defensive. Just
as he must have been all those years ago when he had
been a little boy longing for the kind of mother the other
boys had, yet in the end rejoicing in the eccentricities
that made her so very individual. Again she felt a stab of
something like compassion, surely the very last emotion
one would think of in connection with Daniel Bohun.
Her eyes were caught by a tiny gilt clock on the mantelpiece above the glowing electric fire, and her eyes
widened in sudden panic. Half an hour, Madeleine had
said. She must hurry.

In the end she needn't have because they all had to
wait twenty minutes for their hostess to put in an appearance.

'Maddy!' Daniel went to the staircase twice and
shouted up to her, then came back to where Pierre and
Bianca were on their second glasses of sherry, but each
time he was smiling, shaking his head in affectionate
exasperation when he returned. 'I should have warned
you, Bianca. Being late is one of Mother's minor faults.'
He drained his glass and put it down on the coffee table
around which they were sitting. 'Pierre can probably tell
you a whole lot more.'

'Now I wouldn't say that, Daniel. No, I wouldn't. Not
really.' In spite of his name, Pierre turned out to be an
Irishman, small as a jockey and with the seamed, sea-
soned skin of a recumbent gnome. Bianca watched,
listening with fascination as he nodded his head in

apparent contradiction of what he was saying. 'She has one or two wee foibles. The same as the rest of us, I'm thinking.'

'Whose foibles are you talking about?' Maddy appeared suddenly in the doorway, buckling a beautiful filigree gilt belt about the waist of her black dress, then she looked up and smiled ravishingly at her son. 'Was that you roaring up the stairs, Daniel?' She too seemed to have adopted a touch of Irish brogue. 'I was hurrying as much as I could.'

'Then, please,' he begged, 'may we go in to dinner, darling? I'm starving and I'm sure Bianca is, too.'

'Of course, of course. That's the idea, isn't it? And surely it's best to come to the table when you're anxious to eat? Especially Pierre's divine food.' She slipped a hand through her son's arm, allowing Pierre to escort Bianca, but before they moved in the direction of the dining-room, she paused, looking with pleasure at the younger woman, at the glossy copper-coloured hair curling about her shoulders, the slender figure dressed in a green velvet pinafore under which she wore a wide-sleeved white blouse. 'You look quite lovely, Bianca. I hope my son has told you so.'

'As a matter of fact, Mother, I have.'

Bianca's eyes met his as he spoke, both of them aware only of the other, and they missed the slightly astonished expression on Madeleine's face as she looked at her son, then with a slight shrug she turned towards Pierre. 'Shall we go?' Her tone was soft, wistful, indulgent.

Bianca decided the meal was one of the best she had ever eaten and when she expressed her opinion she saw Pierre shrug his thin shoulders and look complacent.

'Well,' he got up to remove the plates from which they had eaten the rich concoction of meat, vegetables, herbs and wine, 'since I trained in France, I should be able to cook. But as well as that it's a hobby of mine.' After the stew they had cheese and fruit which, with the brook trout grilled for the first course, made a memorable meal.

'There, Daniel,' when they were drinking coffee, it seemed perfectly natural when Madeleine accepted the cheroot her son offered. 'Wasn't it worth a little waiting?'

'Of course it was. I knew it would be and that was what made me more impatient. But,' he took his mother's fingers and touched them to his lips, 'I suppose there's no use expecting you to change now, is there?'

'No use at all, my dear.' She blew the smoke over his head in a gesture of defiance and self-mockery. 'Although I never admit to growing old, I'm much too old to change.'

The rest of the weekend passed in the same easy-going, comfortable atmosphere. Bianca and Daniel went on long country walks and came back to eat Pierre's delicious food with which they seemed always to consume an inordinate amount of wine. Afterwards Bianca wondered if she had passed the days in a faintly alcoholic daze. Had she been drunk on the wine? Or had some other intoxicant been at work?

Much of the time Madeleine spent in her studio and on the Saturday afternoon she invited her guest to go along and have a look at some of 'my things' as she called them.

'Of course I know you won't like them. Most people don't. In fact,' there was a mischievous quality about her smile, 'I should hate it if they were wildly popular. It's like when your favourite piece of music is used as an advertisement for canned soup. So,' she pushed back the chair and drained the last of her coffee, 'come along when it suits you, Bianca, and say just what you like about them. Believe me, I can scent pretence a mile away.'

And Madeleine had been quite right. Bianca neither liked nor understood the pieces of sculpture arranged round the walls of the stone barn at the end of the garden. She had left Daniel back in the house where he was trying to contact someone on the telephone and wandered round, struggling to find some sense in the rather ugly pieces of twisted wire and lumps of concrete which formed the basis of the Bohun collection. Madeleine was busy at the far end of the room with what, to Bianca's untutored eye, looked like electric arc welding equipment, the cascade of sparks brilliant as a Guy Fawkes display. It was some time before she paid any attention to Bianca, but at last she switched off the electricity, pushed back her visor and came across the flagstoned floor.

'This—' she pulled off a glove and laid an affectionate hand on something that might have been part of the anti-invasion sea defences in the war, '—this piece was what got me the invitation to Kent University.'

'I see.' Finding it difficult to think of anything intelligent to say, Bianca frowned and stood back, narrowing her eyes in search of perspective. 'What is it called?' The name might give a clue.

'I call it Anagram.'

'Ah,' said Bianca as if a door had been opened. Then she walked on to the next piece. It was while she was trying to find some sense in this that her eye caught sight of a collection of small sculptures on a shelf and she walked over to get a closer look.

'Oh, I love some of these,' she looked quickly behind her. 'Am I allowed to touch, Madeleine?'

'Of course. You won't hurt them.'

Neither could she, because these small pieces were made of smooth marble, worked in some way so that they gave an impression of figures and polished so that they were pleasant to hold. Instinctively Bianca held one against her face, enjoying the cool touch of it on her skin.

'Choose one,' Madeleine commanded.

'Oh, I couldn't.' Hastily she put down the outline of a running child, the one which attracted her above all, which she had picked up several times.

'I mean to give you one.' With professional detachment the older woman took the sculpture and looked at it assessingly. 'Hmm. It's not bad.' She frowned then held it out. 'Please, Bianca,' the dark eyes so like her son's were regarding Bianca with an amused expression, 'I would like you to have this. It would be so much easier than if I decide to give you Anagram.'

'Oh,' Bianca laughed, 'in that case I have no choice, have I? But thank you, Madeleine. Truly, I shall enjoy living with this.'

'That, my dear, is what it's all about.' And she looked pleased.

When Bianca got back to the house she found Daniel coming to fetch her and he adopted a surprised expression when he saw the small figure in her hand. 'So you've been given *that*.' He took it from her, turning it round in his long fingers so that the light shone softly on the pale-coloured marble. 'Nice.' He handed it back, a strange look in his eyes which she found impossible to identify. 'What did you think of the other pieces?'

'We-ell,' Bianca hesitated, 'I found them difficult to understand.'

'Difficult? Well, that at least is an improvement. Most people think they're impossible.'

'Well, impossible then.' She laughed and leaned against him as he put his arm about her, pulling her close as they went along the pathway towards the house. 'She has one which she calls Anagram. I hoped the name might give me a clue, but . . .'

His laugh sounded deep down in his chest, she felt the reverberation of it as he turned her round to face him. 'I'm afraid that's one of her jokes, darling. She's been through all the obvious ones, like enigma, conundrum, paradox. So now she's decided on Anagram? Sometimes I wonder, is she poking fun at us all? Is it a huge con trick, or does she really believe in what she's doing?'

'She seemed to be enjoying herself with that welding kit. I don't think she would do that unless she believed in it.'

'I don't know,' he answered slowly. 'She might just be capable of it. Now,' briefly, tantalisingly, he brushed his mouth against hers, 'go and get a jacket, I'm going to take you for a walk. Then we're coming back to toasted crumpets in front of the fire. And with luck,' his voice dropped, 'we shan't see Mother or Pierre till dinner.'

They left on Sunday just after lunch and had been driving in a contented silence for some time before Bianca turned round to look at Daniel. 'Thank you for taking me with you this weekend. I think your mother is wonderful and I had a marvellous time.'

'Good.' His fingers laced with hers, then before she was aware of what he was doing he had pulled off the road into a picnic area, his arms were about her, and his lips were parting hers almost before he had turned off the engine.

And Bianca, who found his presence always such sweet torment, was instantly consumed by his touch. Today it was as if they had reached a new plane in their relationship. His hands moved over her body with an intimacy and familiarity which would normally have sent warning signals jangling down her spine, but at this moment her only concern was the urgent clamour of her senses, a clamour which was heightened as she slipped her hand inside his jacket to place her fingers close to that impetuously beating heart.

He dropped a trail of kisses from her eyes to her mouth, lingering there for so long that she knew such sensuous delight could only be a delusion. But even when their lips parted, pleasure increased as he buried his face against her throat, his tongue evoking such trembling sensations that a shuddering groan, faint and half-stifled, escaped her parted lips.

'Bianca. Darling.' His caresses became less frantic, more controlled, until at last he held her back against her seat, hands on her shoulders, an expression in his eyes which told her a little of his struggle for composure. 'Bianca.' A rueful smile twisted his lips, and he released her, thrusting an impatient hand through the disordered black hair. 'I suppose I ought to say I'm sorry but that would be untrue. Only this is neither the time nor the place.' As if unable to resist he leaned forward with closed eyes and put his lips against hers, held them still for a moment then brushed them softly, delicately, several times back and forth.

He was unsmiling when he looked at her again, seeing her passion-drugged, wholly agitated appearance which a hand against the warm swell of her breast did nothing to reduce.

'Darling, I meant you to have soft lights and music but

I can't wait any longer. I want you to marry me, Bianca. And soon. Tell me that you will.'

'Wh-what?' Suddenly Bianca was wide awake, all her soft, willing expectancy wiped away by a wave of something approaching panic. What was she doing here? And with Daniel Bohun? Her eyes, wide, nervous, scanned his for some clue to his wholly unexpected proposal but she could find none.

'Darling.' Powerful fingers circled her neck, his touch turning her bones as usual to that melting tenderness, a finger moving on the nape of her neck removing all doubts from her mind. 'Tell me,' his lips moved against her cheek, 'tell me that you'll marry me.'

'Of course,' she breathed, moving her mouth closer to his. 'Tomorrow. If you want, I'll marry you tomorrow.'

CHAPTER SIX

TOMORROW was too soon, that was a conclusion they came to together as they drove back to town. And yet, neither of them wanted to wait.

'Why should we?' Daniel demanded as he drove the car expertly into the confined parking space of the block of flats. 'We've already been waiting long enough. Don't you agree?' His breath was warm against her cheek as he released his seatbelt and turned round to look at her.

'Yes.' Emotion made her voice tremble. 'I've been waiting for ever.'

'Darling.' There was tenderness in the way he spoke, in the way his hands held her face for a moment before he kissed her. 'What are you trying to say?'

'Just that.' She was glad of the darkness which concealed her blush. 'I *have* waited. I'm sorry if that makes me sound like an anachronism.'

'It doesn't,' he whispered hoarsely. 'It makes you sound perfect. But then I knew that already. I only hope,' amusement lightened the slightly fraught atmosphere inside the car, 'that that won't make you impossible to live with, my sweet.'

'Wh-what do you mean?' She was too confused to be able to follow his reasoning.

'I mean, in my business I'm not too used to coming across perfection—I'm wondering if I can cope.'

'Oh, Daniel.' She found that she could enjoy his teasing. 'I'm not really perfect.' And that she could respond. 'Nearly, but not quite!'

'Then,' he sighed, 'I'll just have to settle for that. Now,' an expert mouth parted hers but briefly, 'I suppose we'd better go upstairs. What do you think Elspeth will have to say about our news?'

'I have the feeling that Elspeth will not be the least bit surprised.'

'Oh?' In the darkness one eyebrow was raised in astonishment. 'How come she knows so much?'

'That,' said Bianca as she got out of the car, 'is a long story and I'll tell you about it some time.'

'More and more intriguing.' He pulled her close as they hurried across to the foyer. 'And what about your sister?'

'She'll be stunned.' She stopped in the shadowy hall, stood on tiptoe and reached her arms about his neck. 'Almost as stunned as I am. But she'll be pleased. I'm sure she and Lex will be very pleased, don't you?'

'Yes.' There was a hint of dryness in his voice that made her look at him more carefully. 'I believe you're right.'

And they were both correct in their expectations of the reception their news would bring. Elspeth was delighted but there was some smugness in the look she gave her friend as she offered her congratulations and when Daniel pressed her she refused to be drawn.

Cindy was even more predictable because from the other end of the telephone came a gasp that could have been heard several feet away.

'You're engaged to—whom?' Even in unforeseeable circumstances Cindy seldom lost her cool.

'To Daniel Bohun.' She shrugged and smiled at the man who was sitting opposite her, holding the receiver towards him so that he could hear Cindy's excited calling for her husband.

Then Lex came on the telephone, his reaction showing all the enthusiasm and more that she would have expected from her announcement. And beneath all the approval, all the extravagant good wishes, there was some other response being carefully concealed. What could it be? When she put down the telephone there was a faint frown on her face, one that made Daniel get up and come across to perch on the arm of her chair.

'What's wrong, my sweet? Don't tell me Lex has forbidden the marriage.'

'No.' In genuine amusement she laughed up into his face. 'Quite the reverse in fact. They're both delighted. Only—' she shrugged her shoulders, determined to dismiss her foolish imaginings. Why on earth should Lex be *relieved* that she was going to be married? 'Only you would think my dear brother-in-law was anxious to get me off his hands at last.' There was a contented sigh as she allowed him to pull her even closer against him. 'I suppose,' she murmured as she held her lips up to his, 'I ought to go and help Elspeth to make tea, but . . .'

Even three weeks was a ridiculously short time to complete all the arrangements. With only days to go, Bianca wondered why she hadn't insisted on another week. But she knew the answer to that before she finished posing the question. Simply because she *couldn't* wait any longer, of course. She didn't *want* to wait. There was no *reason* for them to wait. So after today she would be leaving the office for the three weeks holiday she had, by some fantastic stroke of luck, been saving. Of course, the company would have been accommodating, but she preferred not to have to ask for too many favours.

And she was glad that for a time at least she was going to be able to come back to work at Fantasque. That had rather surprised her and she had even been a little diffident about suggesting to Daniel that she would like to go on working. Somehow, and she had to confess she had been wrong, she had got the idea that he would have had old-fashioned views about wives working. But quite the reverse. In fact he had been most insistent that she should *not* give up her job until she had had more time to think about it.

'In the next few months,' he had told her, 'I'll have to be rushing about the continent on business. I don't think you quite realise,' he broke off to view her with a faintly reproving look, 'just how chaotic my life has become since I met you. My secretary has been giving me some very strange sidelong glances when I've insisted on cancelling *another* important meeting and I've a whole reputation to try to redeem once we get back from our honeymoon. Lots of ruffled feathers will have to be expensively smoothed.'

'I'm sorry.' Her meekness, although far from genuine was amazingly enjoyable. 'Am I right in thinking that you're blaming me?'

'Absolutely right.' His arms about her waist tightened menacingly. 'I'm holding you entirely responsible. You've been shameless in the way you've diverted me from my work and that's why when we come back I'm going to have to leave you far more than I'll be inclined to do. Just for a little while, until I catch up with all the boring, humdrum necessities of life. You *could* come with me, of course, but I'm not going to inflict that on you. You know how meetings can drag on and I would get uptight thinking of you hanging about in some hotel room waiting, impatiently I hope, for me to get back.'

An increase of pressure in her arms about his neck, a few incoherent little murmurs, gave him some idea just how trying she would find such a situation and it was some time before Daniel continued.

'No,' it took some resolution on his part to return to the discussion, 'I would be much happier if I could think of you going to work as usual. I know how much you love your job, all the trappings of success,' he teased, 'rubber plants and your own loo. You've worked hard for it and I'm not going to let you give it up just so you can stay at home and wash my shirts. There'll be time enough for you to decide whether you would rather be at home than dashing out every morning. But I won't deny that I hope eventually, in the not *too* distant future that you will want to stay at home—for one reason or another.' And the implication of those particular words made her heart beat so rapidly that she had no breath, nor inclination for further comment.

But now Daniel was in Europe for a few days tying up some ends before they flew off to a mystery destination for their honeymoon. He had been very evasive about where they were going, teasing her with conflicting comments about insurance cover against the possibility of breaking a leg in some Pyrenean skiing resort and the difficulty of finding sun-filter cream in London in mid-November. But in the end he had relented to the extent of telling her to pack more than one bikini.

She had missed him dreadfully in the last five days and was longing for Thursday when he expected to be back. And Friday would be hectic, taking the last of her belongings from her flat to his, and on Saturday they would be married. She sighed dreamily, then shook herself as she stretched out a hand for another letter from her tray. She really must get on and get all these things dealt with before tonight. She did want an easy mind before she set off on her honeymoon. There I go again, she reprimanded. Talk about a one-track mind!

'Hello.' She stretched out a hand and flicked the buzzer which had drawn her attention. 'What is it, Jane?'

'Someone to see you, Miss Hill. Miss Galston.'

For the moment the name meant nothing. 'Who?'

'Miss Freddie Galston.'

'Oh.' For no reason that she could think of Bianca felt as if she had had a blow in her stomach. There was an almost overwhelming inclination to refuse to see the girl, to say she was too busy and would she come back in, say, four weeks. But she heard her voice replying automatically, 'All right, Jane. Tell her to come in, will you?'

She had only a few seconds to compose herself, not nearly enough, but there was time for her early suspicions to reassert themselves. When she had asked him, Daniel's response to her queries about his relationship with the air stewardess had been too vague to be satisfactory. It was hard to believe that any man would be totally impervious to a girl as beautiful, as sophisticated, as Freddie Galston, and with the best will in the world there was still a tiny niggle of jealousy deep down in her psyche. She . . . Her musings broke off as there was a light tap at the door and Freddie Galston sauntered into the room.

'Hello.' With a deliberate air of distraction Bianca waved a hand vaguely in the direction of the chair pulled closed to the far side of her desk. 'I shan't keep you a minute.' She frowned over the papers she held in her hand, made some careful pencil jottings on a large graph on her desk, details which she knew she would be obliged to erase the moment her visitor had gone, and all the time she was conscious of the lounging figure of the girl opposite. That first cursory look had confirmed her opinion, dismissing any idea that her memory might have been playing her tricks.

Freddie was wearing a figure-hugging pants suit in a deep shade of blue which almost matched her eyes and clung lovingly to her tall slender figure. A white polo-neck jumper showed off her lightly tanned skin and her blonde hair was immaculately pulled into a french pleat at the back of her head. When Bianca looked up she was rummaging in her red suede shoulder-bag from which she extracted a gold cigarette case. Bianca declined when it was offered to her and watched with mounting agitation and annoyance as the girl appeared to take her time about lighting up. At last she felt obliged to speak and immediately felt she had given away the advantage of being on home ground.

'I can give you only a few moments.' Bianca glanced at her watch. 'I have a lot to do.'

'Oh, yes.' Freddie smiled showing small, very white and even teeth. 'I did hear.' Mockery was in her tones. 'It's Saturday, isn't it? The great day?'

'Yes.' Bianca wondered if she had visibly paled. How had Freddie heard? She and Daniel had been very discreet, both determined on a quiet wedding with only their closest friends present.

'Is it possible?' Freddie's manner had subtly changed, her voice was now coloured by a pseudo-sympathy. 'Is it possible that you haven't seen through it all?'

'I don't know what you're talking about.' Intuition requiring an urgent reason for getting rid of her visitor as soon as possible made Bianca get to her feet. 'And I really haven't time for anything personal at the moment.' She forced a laugh but knew it had not for a moment deceived the other woman. 'So I think I must ask you to . . .'

'Do you really think Daniel has any intention of turning up on Saturday?'

Bianca whirled round from her filing cabinet, one hand going to her throat in a defensive gesture. Now she knew that all colour had drained from her face. Not that it mattered. 'Would you please go now.' Her hands were shaking as she forced herself back to look through her records. 'I must get on.'

'I've come simply because I'm sorry for you.'

Bianca closed her eyes for a moment then forced herself to turn and face her adversary. 'Sorry for me!' Her laugh had an edge of hysteria. 'Are you sure you're not simply jealous?'

'Maybe.' Freddie smiled with an air of frankness difficult to dismiss. 'I have been a bit annoyed,' she shrugged disarmingly and smiled, 'jealous then, I'll admit it, of all the time he's spent with you in the last weeks. Only, I think he's going a bit too far. Even for Daniel.'

Bianca stood silent, unable to respond to her inclination to run into her private cloakroom, lock the door and not emerge until she knew that her unwelcome visitor had gone. Instead she was rooted to the spot, forced against her will to listen to what the other girl was saying.

'Believe me, I know Daniel much better than you do.' Her eyes narrowed and she blew smoke away from her in an elegant puff. 'He's utterly charming and utterly ruthless. And he hates anything that makes him look anything other than in complete control. I've told him it's something to do with his unconventional upbringing.' She smiled amiably. 'If you've met Maddy you'll understand why. From that first moment when you cut him like that in front of all the cameras at the airport, he was determined to get his own back on you.'

'Did he tell you that?' Bianca's lips were stiff.

'Oh, he didn't at first. All he did was ask me to find out who had been sitting in the adjoining seat. Of course it's against the rules, but,' she shrugged, 'rules are always being broken. The funny thing is that I didn't recognise you that day we met at Lex's. It wasn't until we were driving back to London that something clicked and I remembered where I had seen you.'

'Oh.' She was too stunned to utter more than the meaningless monosyllable.

'Then of course he's always had it in for your sister.'

'Cindy? What do you mean?'

'Well, the first Mrs Comyn is a great friend of his and I imagine deep down he has always blamed your sister for breaking up the marriage.'

'But . . .' It was impossible for her to go on.

'Oh, I know, it's too ridiculous. Too unkind.' Freddie's voice was simply oozing sympathy now. 'That's why I thought it only fair to let you know what was going to happen. He can be a real devil at times. And, I know how I would feel if I were actually jilted.'

'Jilted?' Bianca's head came up with a jerk, trying to see why that particular word had been used. Had Daniel actually told Freddie how he had put a stop to that earlier romance. Had he laughed when he had let her know that it wouldn't be the first but . . .

'Well, I always think it's better to call a spade a spade, don't you?' With a sigh she got to her feet. 'I'm sorry to have been the one to tell you, but I've done it now.' She spoke as if she had found it an unpleasant duty which she was relieved to have dealt with. 'Whatever action you take now is up to you.' The smile that came to her lips faltered as she looked at Bianca's ashen face, but quickly she bent down to pick her handbag up from the chair.

'Well—I'd better go. I suppose there are things you have to think about.' But even when she had her hand on the doorknob she was reluctant to go, there was one more round in her gun. 'I should try not to let it worry you *too* much. I told Daniel last night . . .

'Last night?' The question would not be stopped.

'Yes. I was with him last night in Luxemburg and . . .'

'Please go.' Bianca just managed to hold on to her control. She looked away from the elegant figure standing in front of the door and missed the expression, quickly veiled, of sheer triumph on her face. A moment later the door closed silently behind her.

She had no idea how long she sat there staring into space, unable to think of anything but the terrible pain in her chest. In fact she was unaware of the cause of the discomfort, only that it was unbearable. Some devious instinct made her take advantage of Jane's usual absence from her office at that time of day to run down to the street and hail a passing taxi. Then she lay back in the corner shivering uncontrollably while she was driven back to her flat.

Elspeth had gone away for a few days, not being due back in London until the morning of the wedding, and Bianca knew that if she had been there it would have been impossible for her to return home. What she would have done she didn't know, but sympathy and advice would have been intolerable.

She sat in total darkness in the sitting-room for several hours, endeavouring to control the pain, then when that had been achieved the bitterness of what she had learned threatened to swamp her. The greatest agony of all was her lack of disbelief. It all fitted in too neatly to allow a second's comfort. She had only to think back to that day when he had become a bit uptight about her perfectly natural suggestion that his mother should be informed about the wedding.

'Don't let it worry you, Bianca.' She had sensed that he was struggling to hide his irritation. 'I've told you Maddy won't mind. She loathes weddings and always ignores invitations.'

'But still,' she was not reassured, 'you're her only son and I wouldn't want her to think . . . She was so kind to me that weekend. At least we must let her know then she can decide herself whether or not she comes to the wedding.'

'In any case, I've no idea where she is at the moment. She's gone off to the States, but she's not due at the university till the end of the month. She could be with any number of a score of people, and I certainly don't know all the addresses. But I tell you what, darling,' he came and sat on the arm of her chair, tilting her chin and smoothing away the frown from her forehead. 'we'll take a quick trip out there as soon as possible. She would enjoy that much more. How does that suit you?'

'Well . . .' Bianca sighed. 'I still think . . . And besides, I shan't be able to take any more time off work. It's just by chance that I have saved up these three weeks.'

'Don't worry about that.' Sensing victory, his irritation seemed to be flowing away, he dropped his head so their cheeks were touching, a position that robbed her of any ability to reach decisions as he no doubt knew. 'If I want you to take some more time off I'll just have to speak to Cyrus J. and tell him that I need to borrow his chief consultant for a week or two.'

'Oh, don't do that, Daniel. I would rather arrange these things for myself.'

'Of course, my sweet.' He rose rather abruptly leaving her with the impression of having said something to annoy him. 'Isn't that why you're keeping on your job. Because I want you to arrange these things for yourself.' And he had changed the subject with a finality which would have infuriated the mildest of women's libbers.

Yes, Daniel Bohun had been a cruel hard-hearted devil all those years ago when he had come between Simon and herself, caring nothing for her. She had hated him, had sworn to hate him for the rest of her life. Only, she had forgotten that vow, had allowed herself to be beguiled after that first public demonstration. And that was what had brought all his wrath down on her head.

Yes, she believed all that Freddie had told her even though she wasn't certain she had been told everything. He might not have told about the romance with Simon. In fact, it seemed likely that he had kept that to himself, if he had spoken about it she was fairly certain the other girl would have found her knowledge irresistible. For some reason, in the dark recesses of Daniel Bohun's mind, he still wanted to punish her for what had happened all those years ago.

Hours later, Bianca realised she was shivering and put a match to the gas fire in the sitting-room. She dropped to her knees in front of the flames, holding her hands out in an appealing way. Then she found her way into the kitchen and made herself some tea.

Gradually as she sipped it and some warmth began to creep back to her chilled bones, she realised that anger was the only thing that was going to save her. Anger and desire to strike first, to strike hard, were the only things which could cauterise the pain which was threatening to swamp her entire body.

She returned to the sitting-room and sat down again in front of the fire, her brain searching furiously for some solution. And gradually, she decided on a plan that would allow her to escape the humiliation he had planned for her. The wide mouth curved in a smile of satisfaction. But there was bleakness in her eyes, ice in her heart.

The next day was a wild rush of planning and execution demanding a clear head which was something she did not have. It had been unwise to 'borrow' from Elspeth's dressing-table drawer two of the prescribed sleeping pills she had taken for a short time after her fiancé left on his round-the-world trip. Unwise and yet inevitable for without them she would have been unable to sleep a wink, and the short oblivion had been very sweet.

But the day once it started had been frantic. Booking for a package holiday in Israel was simple enough, although she had no idea why she had chosen that particular country. In fact the clerk in the travel agency had given her a funny look when she had insisted in a sub-hysterical voice that it didn't matter where it was so long as it was a tour with a crowded itinerary.

'Well,' the young man turned the brochure round so she could check for herself, 'as you can see there's only two half days in Tel Aviv, the rest of the time you're either on a coach or flying between resorts.' He smiled encouragingly. 'It's not a tour for the faint-hearted, madam.'

That and the fact that she would be leaving London Airport tonight clinched the matter for her. This way she would be out of the country before he came back. In her mind his name had been obliterated, she thought of him only as 'he'.

Luckily her passport was in order and there were only a few things to be thrown into a case. None of the clothes she had chosen with such trembling excitement for 'him' would be included. They would stay in her wardrobe and when she came back home she would be able to deal with them.

She thought she was feeling better by teatime. That quivering anxiety seemed to have left her, she was totally calm, suffering from shock if she had but known. But more from force of habit than from any interest, she drank a cup of coffee and ate a sandwich while waiting for her taxi.

She saw the explanatory letters on the mantelpiece and that curiously enough brought a sting of tears to her eyes. How disappointed Elspeth would be. And Cindy, too, but she hoped they would understand. It would have been better if she could have phoned to tell them, but she knew that if she spoke to anyone the tears would begin and would never stop. It would be more civilised to let them have the letters, much less upsetting for all of them than a face to face or a telephone confrontation. She knew that if she had had to speak about what had happened to *anyone* she would suffer a total breakdown. All that was keeping her going was the idea that in some perverse way it was *she* who was opting out. When she stopped thinking of that her whole world would crumble.

The ringing of the doorbell brought her back to what was immediate and she walked through to the hall, swung the suede jacket from the coat rack and slipped her hands into the sleeves. 'Coming,' she called, bending to pick up her case and handbag as she moved towards the door.

Then with a thrill of anxiety she drew in her breath, turned back to the small hall table and picked up the passport and tickets which she had forgotten earlier to put into her bag. The thought of arriving at the airport desk with neither of these important documents made the hair on the nape of her neck stand on end. She gave a rueful glance in the mirror above the table, noticing with detachment that her eyes were enormous in her white face, that even the discreet touch of lipstick stood out garishly.

She held the ticket between her teeth while she endeavoured to pull open her handbag zip which seemed to have jammed. Holding the case, handbag and passport did nothing to simplify the task and she frowned with irritation when at that very moment the doorbell rang again, this time with more insistence than it had before.

'Blast,' she muttered through teeth and ticket, dropping the case and turning the handle of the door so that it swung open. And there, on the doorstep, was not the taxi-driver she expected to greet. *He* was there, the very last person in the world she wanted to see, the very man all this charade had been designed to help her to escape from.

'Bi-anca!' That look had been in his face, the one that in other circumstances would have made her melt with longing for him. But even as he spoke her name he changed, the dark eyes searching her face and figure relentlessly, picking up clues which brought a watchfulness to his expression, a slight hardening of his features.

Without saying another word he stepped inside so that she was forced to retreat a step if she wished to avoid physical contact. He pushed the door closed with his foot, still keeping his eyes on her face, making her conscious that stupidly she was still holding the ticket between her teeth, the passport clearly visible as she continued what seemed to be a doomed struggle with the fastener.

At once her hand went up and she tried to be casual in her removal of the ticket, but it was impossible to submit to that hard continuous scrutiny so she looked down at her fingers, busy with the handbag. At last the zip yielded but before she could push her things inside, away from his sight, the doorbell shrilled suddenly with an insistence that would not be denied.

Daniel reached behind him, turned the knob and opened the door, only then removing his eyes from hers and swinging round to cast a baleful eye on the taxi-driver who stood there.

'Evening, guv.' He looked from one silent figure to the other. 'Party here for London Airport?'

Bianca swallowed, wishing she had the strength to push Daniel aside and go with the taxi-driver, but she knew too well that was something he would never allow. He was determined to have his own way. Freddie had said that. And ruthless, she had said. Seeing the expression in the eyes that flicked from the puzzled taxi-driver on the doorstep to herself, she knew that there had been no exaggeration. He would never permit her to go without an explanation. And, she felt exultant at the thought of such a total revenge, perhaps it was as well to take the opportunity that had so unexpectedly presented itself and to give it now.

'There's been a change of plans.' He turned to the man on the step and Bianca heard the rustle of notes changing hands. 'I'm sorry you've been troubled.'

'No trouble, guv.' The tip had apparently been large enough to console. ''Night, then.'

The door closed once again, and Daniel turned slowly, reluctantly to face her. His hand came out to take the airline ticket from her fingers and she made no attempt to stop him. He flicked through the pages noting the details then, with a tightening of his lips, looked up again.

'Why?' The dark eyes had a flinty colour, his mouth looked thin, lips were held tightly over his teeth. Then there was an easing of his expression, and he walked away from her in the direction of the sitting-room, leaving her no choice but to follow. Bianca watched him throw himself into a chair and a welcome surge of resentment whipped still more violent feelings against him. Coldly she took in details of the dark suit under the light camel overcoat, the silk shirt and red Paisley-pattern tie. Oh yes, it was going to be very pleasant taking this man down a few pegs, letting him know that he wasn't the only one capable of playing a double game.

'Why, Bianca?' There was a shade more force in his tone now, reminding her that if she did not provide an answer then there was a chance that he might be prepared to shake one from her. She shivered but hoped her slight, casual shrug would conceal it from him.

'Why?' Her voice was lighter than she would have dared to hope. 'You ask me that. You, of all people!'

His eyes narrowed further, but his voice showed none of the anger she was certain he must be feeling. 'Yes. I am asking you to explain. And I don't want some cryptic answer that could mean anything or nothing. I'm asking,' he unfolded his length from the chair and stood over her, hands thrust into the pockets of his coat, 'what is going on? Why do I come home and find you apparently about to fly off to,' he pulled the ticket from his pocket and flicked it open, 'to Tel Aviv? When the arrangement was that you and I were to be married on Saturday. And I hope you're not going to tell me,' in his voice was an edge of bitter amusement, 'that you were going for only one night.'

For an absurd instant Bianca thought there had been a mistake. She couldn't feel like this, her body washed by waves of longing for him, not if she hated him at the same time. It was too much of a wild contradiction. And then she remembered, Freddie had spent the night with him. Jealousy tore at her as she imagined them in each other's arms and she was reminded of her loathing.

'No.' It was an effort to keep her voice steady. 'I'm not going to tell you that. If you study the ticket you'll see that it's a fourteen-day tour of the Holy Land.' She glanced at the clock on the mantelpiece. 'I haven't much time. The flight leaves about ten.'

But his eyes had followed hers and when she looked back at him it was to see him move towards the fire. He stood for a minute looking at the two prominently displayed letters, one addressed to Elspeth, the other to Cindy. He picked up Elspeth's, studied it for a moment, then turned back to her, flicking the envelope against his fingertips once or twice.

'You were saying,' his eyes drifted over her features. 'something about me. Of all people.'

'Yes. You of all people.' She had gained a little more confidence. 'Why should you of all people be surprised when a marriage doesn't take place? Aren't you something of an expert at that?' The last words she almost spat at him then turned abruptly away from him to hide the glitter of tears in her eyes.

'Are you telling me,' his voice was low with menace, 'that you planned all this just so you could pay me back . . .'

'It was so tempting.' Her feelings were under control again and she felt it safe to face him with a slight laugh. 'I suppose I ought to feel guilty, but I don't. All I have to do is remember just what I suffered when you stopped me marrying Simon. That seemed to give me the right.'

'So,' there was a smile on his lips, something she hadn't expected, but there was a cruel twist which caused a shiver of fear, 'you've decided and that's the end of it.' From the inside pocket of his jacket he pulled out a slim gold case, extracted a cheroot and lit it. His action reminded her of Freddie, and fanned her already hot anger.

'That's right!' she snapped.

'Is it?' His eyes never left her face and he made no effort now to conceal the contempt he felt for her, but he spoke in the slow lazy drawl which once upon a time she had found so affecting. 'Is it, Bianca?' There was more than a trace of black humour in his words, enough to make Bianca doubt the wisdom of her carefully conceived scheme, enough to make her feel an urgent need to finish this scene and get off to the airport. In any case, panic began to mount in her. If she didn't get a move on she would miss her flight—all that money down the drain, she thought, as she stepped across to the telephone and began to dial a number.

She had reached the last digit when his hand came down, firmly obliterating her call, and she whirled round at him, knocking his hand away as if she could not bear to have it near her. A sob forced itself from her lips as with shaking finger she began again.

'What do you think you're doing?' His voice was icy.

'I'm calling a taxi. What do you think! If I don't get to the airport, I'm going to miss my flight.'

'Oh, Bianca.' He spoke to her as if she were a child, one who had behaved atrociously but with whom the adult was endeavouring to be patient. 'You don't really imagine that I'm going to let you walk out on me, do you?'

'Wh-what do you mean?' For a moment a spark of optimism flared only to be extinguished when she saw the hard line of his mouth.

'I mean,' almost gently he took the receiver from her and replaced it in the cradle, 'that you aren't going anywhere. At least not tonight.' To underline the point in the most dynamic way possible he took the booklet of tickets and tore them across, then again, and put them into a large glass ashtray and touched the pieces with the flame from his lighter. At that moment, too, it seemed that he had had enough of tobacco for he ground out his cigar among the debris of the ticket. Bianca watched him in impotent fury, wishing she could give way to her instincts which were to kick and spit and scratch but instead she spoke, hoping that her voice showed how much she despised him.

'That doesn't matter. Not in the least. So what?' She shrugged and turned away from him. 'I'm not the least bit interested in a holiday in Israel. It just happened to be the lesser of two evils.'

'Really?' He allowed himself a bleak little smile and Bianca felt another shiver start at the base and run up her spine. It was true what Freddie had said, she was sure he could be a real devil if he wanted. 'Well, it's a great pity, my love. For you're going to have to endure the greater of the two evils, whether you like it or not.'

For a moment Bianca couldn't think what he meant. This way of getting back at her had come into none of her plans, it hadn't been catered for in any of the scenes she had enacted last night. He was even worse than she had thought, prepared to go to any lengths to save his precious pride. Not that he could force her of course, and her lip curled with satisfaction as she threw the words back at him.

'*I'll* have to endure,' she jeered, 'how amusing! Do you think there's any power on earth that can *make* me marry if I don't want to?'

She drew in a breath as he stepped towards her and took her by the shoulders, shaking her none too gently. Fear seared through Bianca's veins as she wondered if perhaps she had gone too far. What was to stop him doing anything he wanted? She could be left here as lifeless as a rag doll and . . .

'Do you think I'm prepared to put up with anything you like to dish out.' Another shake and he allowed her to collapse into a chair where she lay looking up at him, wondering where her clever plan had gone so hideously wrong.

'You've no choice.' Her manner was less assured than it had been. You can't make me do anything I don't . . .' Her voice trailed away.

For a long time he stood staring down at her, hatred and contempt in every feature. Bianca wondered why she should feel so wounded at such a natural expression of feelings, but then she noticed a faint smile curve the mouth although the expression of the eyes continued like shale on a bleak mountain.

'Can't I, Bianca?' His voice was silky, lover-like except for the underlying current of animosity. 'Can't I?' Almost negligently he bent towards her, caught her hands in his and with a savage jerk pulled her back to her feet. Her heart was hammering in a most uncomfortable way and she had to bend backwards to put as much distance between her face and his as was possible. Only the lower parts of their bodies were in close proximity; she was uncomfortably aware of his hands going about her waist, sliding down her hips as he moulded her more closely against him. He smiled down at her for a moment, and laughed aloud as she jerked her face sideways with an expression of distaste.

'Do you really think I'd allow you to make such a fool of me, Bianca?'

'I-I don't know.' You were prepared to make a fool of me, she screamed silently, only her pride would not allow her to utter the words. 'But in any case—' She struggled briefly against the relentless pressure of his hands then gave up. Possibly now was the time to be conciliatory, for her own safety. 'But in any case, hardly anyone knows so . . .' It seemed a weak comment and she allowed it to die away.

'Everyone who matters knows. And in any event I understand that our "happy news",' he made it sound like a killer disease, 'will be released in one of the page three scoops tomorrow. I wonder,' he grinned down at her knowingly, 'I just wonder who let them know, Bee.' He mocked her with the name. 'Is it possible that the bride just happened to ring someone so that her disappearance on the morning of the wedding would be *that* much more of a sensation..'

'No, of course not. Why should I do that?' She struggled again but his strength was inexorable. 'I didn't mean . . .'

'You protest too much, my dear. But,' suddenly his arms released her and at the same time any pretence of amusement disappeared from his face, 'it no longer matters. The whole thing has gone too far. You will be at the register office on Saturday morning. You will go through the farce of a wedding whether it suits you now or not. Do you understand?'

Bianca felt hysteria rise inside her but she fought against it, and turned away from him with a contemptuous little shrug of the shoulder.

'No way.' As they say in all the most elegant of places.

But before the words were more than out of her mouth, she felt herself whirled round again to face him and this time there was no mistaking the savagery in his face or his voice.

'Then if you don't, be prepared to see your sister ruined.'

If there was any colour in her cheeks, Bianca felt it leave them in that minute. She felt every drop of blood drain away so that the room began to whirl about her. No supporting hand came out to sustain her, no tender enquiry was made, so in the end she forced the nausea away and gradually his figure, larger and more menacing than before, materialised in front of her.

'Wh-What did you say?' If there was any appeal in the shaking hand that went up to push the hair back from her face, then he was left unmoved.

'You heard me.' His tone was brutal, uncaring.

'You said, something . . . Cindy. Ruined.'

'She and her husband.' He gave a short laugh and subsided again on to the chair, looking, she thought with fatalistic anger, more relaxed, as if now assured that he had regained his total control.

'What do you mean?' Her legs were refusing to support her and she slipped down on to the arm of a chair.

'I mean—' She would have liked in some violent way to wipe the enjoyment off his face. 'I mean, my dear Bee, that if you refuse to turn up on Saturday morning *and* play the part of the willing, tremulous bride, then both Lex and your sister are very likely to see the inside of a prison. I suppose it's possible,' he considered thoughtfully, 'that your nephew might even be born inside. But no!' he frowned, 'the case would be unlikely to come up in that time. It will need at least two years investigation by the Fraud Squad.'

Bianca lay back on the chair staring at him. She doubted not a word that he had said to her. Things seemed to have a habit of slotting in. Little things which had made her curious, now became clear. She had known for a long time that Lex and Cindy were worried about something.

'So you see,' Daniel seemed amused by the entire situation now, 'I have every confidence that you will appear on Saturday morning, and just to underline my faith in you,' he smiled as he picked up the passport which had been tossed on to the coffee table, 'I'll take care of this. Without it,' there was a sudden blaze in the depths of his eyes, 'we would be unable to set off on that luxury honeymoon.' He bent and brushed cold lips with his, in a joyless but total mark of ownership. 'It looks like it's to be a sentence whichever way you look at it. For them. Or for us. It's up to you, my sweet.'

CHAPTER SEVEN

SHE hoped there could be no mistaking the hatred, sheer
and untinged by any weaker emotion, in the eyes that
stared back at him. If only she could disbelieve. Lex
perhaps. But Cindy . . .? And yet there was that confidence about Daniel that dispelled any lingering hope.
With an attempt at ease she swung her legs round, sat up
in her seat, hands on the arms, head supported by the
back in an attempt at defiance.

'Do you really expect me to believe what you say?'

'I'm not really interested.' He shrugged and smiled
pleasantly as if they were having an ordinary discussion.

'But . . . even if what you say is true, what can *you* do
about it? You're not God Almighty with the power to
exact vengeance.' The simile seemed too apt for her own
case and she caught her lower lip between her teeth.

'No, I'm not God Almighty, but I do happen to be the
only person who is interested in buying Comyn International. My accountants have been burrowing away for
months and have come up with some very disturbing
reports. There's no doubt about it, I'm afraid, Lex and
your sister have been up to some very unethical tricks
and . . .'

'Lex maybe.' Her doubts burst out before she could
stop them. 'But not Cindy. Never Cindy!'

'Your loyalty does you great credit,' he said sarcasti-
cally, 'but I'm afraid in this instance it's entirely mis-
placed. She wouldn't be the first private secretary to help
her boss to cook the books and when she's his . . .' there

120

was the merest hesitation on which she knew was intentional, 'wife as well . . .'

Bianca remembered Freddie had spoken of Lex's first marriage. Another small piece fell into place, and all her confident defiance ebbed nearly away. 'Why should I bother to save them?'

'That,' he said smoothly, 'is what I am asking myself, my dear. But somehow, I know that you will.'

There was a short silence broken by a stifled sigh from him, and he shot back his cuff, frowned down at his wrist watch and turned to the door.

'I *did* come round to take you out to dinner, but in the circumstances that seems inappropriate. I'm going back to the flat but I'll be round in the morning to pick up your things.' He spoke as if the entire matter had been settled to their mutual satisfaction.

'I probably won't be here.' It was a final kick of resistance.

'Oh, you'll be here all right.' There was a grim smile about his lips as he studied her with a dispassionate, cynical eye. 'You know exactly what side your . . . or rather your sister's bread is buttered, my dear. I'll be round about ten, I hope that will suit you.' And without waiting for confirmation of that suitability, he left the room and the front door closed firmly a second later.

Bianca lay in the chair for a long time without moving. It no longer seemed to matter that the check-in time for her journey to Israel drew near and passed, her mind was too absorbed in trying to cope with all that had been said to be concerned about an aborted holiday trip. But as hard as she tried, there was no way she could even begin to understand what had happened since she opened the door to what she thought was the taxi-driver.

He was a fiend. With a sob she came to that conclu-

sion, it was the only one that could be reached. Only a
fiend could have turned the tables with such a
vengeance. Only a devil could have arrived at the exact
moment when all the clear evidence was so neatly
offered to him; her obvious flight, the destination clenched so conveniently between her teeth, the taxi-driver
speaking of London Airport. You'd almost have
thought he had been tipped off and yet who . . .?

Freddie of course was the person who sprang immediately to mind, but that was letting her imagination
run riot. No one, no one could have known, and if by
chance Freddie had found some clue, even if she had
guessed, then surely any hint to Daniel had had exactly
the opposite effect from the one Freddie intended—not
sending him rushing back to her but instead determining
him to proceed with something that had started out as a
cruel confidence trick.

That, thinking of how easily she had been manipu-
lated, finally brought the tears that had been dammed up
for nearly thirty hours. Bianca went through to the
bedroom which she had left such a short time before and
threw herself sobbing on to the top cover. After a long
time she fell asleep from sheer exhaustion.

The shrilling of the telephone woke her next morning
and she stumbled through the darkened flat to the
sitting-room, aware of little but the need to stop the
noise. There was a deeper more insistent sense of something wrong, but it wasn't until she heard her sister's
voice that the entire picture flicked back into her mind.

'Hello, darling.' Cindy's voice was careful. 'How's the
bride?'

'The bride?' Bianca forced a laugh. 'Do you mean
me?'

'Who else? How are you, love?'

'I'm fine. But tired.'

'Yes, all the fuss is extremely exhausting. Even a quiet wedding like the one you've insisted on.' There was a pause as if Cindy was composing an important question. 'You haven't been in contact with Daniel this morning, have you, Bianca?'

'No.' She yawned deliberately but her mind was racing with the possibilities of where all this was leading. 'As a matter of fact your call woke me.'

'What?' Cindy sounded shocked. 'And it's nine o'clock!'

'Nine? But it can't be!'

'It is, my dear. But, I, that is Lex,' Bianca could imagine her brother-in-law hovering in the background prompting his wife, 'has been trying to contact Daniel.' An edge of anxiety brought warning signals jangling in her listener's brain. 'You know they're involved in some rather complex business deal at the moment. Well, this morning they were supposed to have been getting together to iron out some final details. But Daniel's secretary rang to say that he would be unable to meet Lex today. I wondered if . . .' she hesitated.

'If what?' Bianca played for time.

'If you knew anything.'

'I know that he's supposed to be collecting me and some of my things about ten.'

'Oh?' Cindy's relief was almost palpable. 'Oh, I see. Of course. Look love, here's Lex. He would like to have a word.' And without more ado, Bianca found herself being interrogated by her brother-in-law who showed none of Cindy's attempts at finesse.

'Bianca, have you any idea why Daniel's called off the meeting I had with him this morning?'

'None at all,' she lied, making no attempt to disguise

the animosity she was beginning to feel. 'Except that last night he told me to be ready when he came round at ten.'

'Why should he tell you ten when he knew perfectly well that he had arranged to meet me then?'

'I can't explain that, Lex. He has told me nothing about his business affairs.' She paused. 'What exactly had you and he planned to do this morning?'

'It's about this merger.' There was a shade of bluster in Lex's manner now. 'We were supposed to be confirming the final agreement today and I would just like to know where we are. It's not very professional to behave like this. A lot depends on . . .'

Bianca suddenly felt sickened of the whole business and interrupted coldly. 'When he arrives I'll let him know how you feel.'

'Well no, don't do that, love.' Lex's manner altered subtly. 'I can quite see,' his laugh was strained, 'that he'll have other things on his mind just now. But with you getting married tomorrow—' He paused as if giving her the opportunity to confirm that and when she did not he went on, 'When you go off on your honeymoon, there'll be no chance of getting things settled till you come back. How long do you think that'll be, love?'

'I'm not sure.' It was impossible for her to keep the note of cynicism from her voice and if it caused Lex some anxiety then she had no regrets. 'It's all a great secret and I'm to be the last one to know. But I do have three weeks holiday.'

'Yes.' He sounded entirely dejected. 'That's what Cindy said.'

'Anyway, I'll tell him that you're a bit anxious.' Mention of her sister reminded Bianca of her main concern. 'How is Cindy keeping? I didn't have the chance to ask her.'

'Oh, she's blooming,' Lex spoke grudgingly, revealing much about his attitude to approaching parenthood. 'D'you want to have another word with her?'

'No, I'll have to go.'

'Well, be discreet about what you say to Daniel, won't you, Bianca? Bad business policy to let people know that you're anxious to clinch a deal. Especially a big deal like selling Comyn International. My own baby, you know!' He laughed but again with that edge of uncertainty. 'See you and Daniel tomorrow then, love. At the registrar's.'

By ten o'clock Bianca was waiting in the hall of the flat for Daniel to arrive. If she had needed any confirmation of the shakiness of the situation her brother-in-law was in their conversation had provided that. Much of Lex's slightly aggressive self-assurance had gone to be replaced by a blustering uncertainty that told her that everything she had heard the previous night was the truth. So...there was no escape for her. If she wanted to save Cindy, Lex she didn't really care about overmuch, then she had no choice but to go ahead with the marriage. Unless, and as the five minutes after ten ticked away she grew increasingly uptight, unless Daniel Bohun had decided he would exact a more satisfying victory if he were to get at her through her sister.

At least that worry disappeared when the doorbell rang with that insistent, imperious note that could presage only one man. She opened the door and they stood for a few seconds staring at each other. His eyes swept over her making her feel glad that she had taken particular care over her appearance. It had been difficult for her to obliterate completely the ravages of the last two days, but she was an expert and was convinced that she had succeeded fairly well. The only clue was the shadowy

darkness beneath her eyes and after a little considera-
tion she decided that that added to an air of fragility
brought about by the crash diet she had embarked on in
preparation for her wedding.

As far as dress was concerned, her velvet trousers in a
particularly attractive shade of cerise were elegantly
efficient, teamed with a silk blouse in pale pink with a
black-and-white scarf knotted at the open neck. Over
this she wore a padded waistcoat in cerise and tur-
quoise-patterned cotton—a warm and suitable outfit for
moving day.

When he closed the door behind him Daniel stood for
a moment, then his eyes moved to the pile of suitcases
and boxes, mostly filled with wedding presents, then
travelled back to her. The jeering raised eyebrow told
her that although he was hardly surprised at her decision, he thought no more of her for it. She coloured
angrily and turned away, but although he was out of her
vision his image was as clearly imprinted as if she were
still looking at him.

At least he gave no indication of disturbance, either
physical or mental—he was his usual confident well-
groomed self, as brutally handsome as ever she told
herself with a tiny shiver of apprehension. She knew just
how he would look when he removed the casual jacket,
undid the navy-and-red-striped tie he was wearing and
pushed up the sleeves of his white shirt. Her stomach
churned at the thought of intimate hours spent in his flat
settling in her things. She remembered the large bedroom which they had planned to share. She hoped he
didn't imagine that now . . . Agitated, she whirled
around to disabuse him of any such idea, but her protest
died when she saw him bending down to assess the
weight of some of the packages. He looked up briefly,

with neither warmth nor intimacy, then immediately back to what he was doing.

'If you can bring some of the lighter packages down, we'll see what we can get in the car. We'll have to make one or two trips.'

'That one's heavy.' It was the first time she had spoken but her voice was as matter-of-fact as his had been. Possibly a shade cooler. 'It's the dinner service.'

'I'll be careful.'

It was only when they reached his flat, having taken the first load up in the lift, that she spoke to him again. And she had to force herself to break the silence that he showed little inclination to end.

'I-I had a telephone call from Lex this morning.'

'Oh yes.' He could hardly have been less interested, not even glancing up to look at her.

'Yes.' His lack of concern made her anger rise. 'He was worried about the fact that your secretary cancelled the meeting you were supposed to be having with him at ten this morning.'

'He would be.' Daniel uncurled his length from the box containing the dinner set which he had just deposited in a corner of the kitchen floor. 'And did you explain to him?' The dark eyes were cruel in their scrutiny of her face, challenging in their indifference to her appearance.

'Of course I didn't!' Her voice was scornful. 'Did you expect me to?'

'I didn't think of it much.' He turned away and walked into the hall to pick up one or two of the smaller packages. 'I don't mind whether you tell him or not. But,' he glanced up at her and smiled without humour, 'if you think Lex Comyn will be too honourable to allow you to make the sacrifice my dear, then don't. I know him a great deal better than you do and I can think of nothing he wouldn't do to save his financial skin. Your "sacrifice" would come very low down on his list.' The statement seemed to afford him a certain amount of satisfaction and Bianca had to resist the temptation to hit him very hard on his smug face. Instead, she took advantage of the opening offered to clear up the matter which had caused her such concern a little time before. She bent down to pick up one of her cases.

'Would you mind showing me where I can put my things?' Her face flamed at the look of amusement on his. 'You *can* force me to marry you, it seems, but you *can't* make me share your bed.' Her heart was hammering wildly as she waited for what seemed a long time for his answer.

'I disagree with you.' His denial caused her agitation to increase, as did the lazy way his eyes moved slowly over her body, lingering she thought at where her heart seemed to be fluttering against the thin silk of her blouse. 'I could make you if I wanted to, but as it happens I don't. There's the other bedroom at the end of the hallway. Use that.'

Bianca felt as if a rug had suddenly been pulled from under her feet but she rallied her spirits quickly. 'Thank you,' she said coldly as she began to walk away. 'I'm particular about who I make love with.'

She didn't hear him move behind her, the thick carpet muffled the sound of his feet, so that his hand on her shoulder whirling her round to face him was a shock which caused her to lose her grip on the case. 'So,' he hissed the word at her and his eyes blazed furiously, 'that too was a lie!'

'Wh—What?' She had a recurrence of the fear she had suffered last night. 'What are you talking about?'

'About you,' he jeered, the anger seeming to have given way to contempt. 'All that waffle about your virtue.'

Bianca felt a flare of satisfaction that at last she had found a way to disconcert him. 'Oh, do me a favour,' she said coolly while she shrugged his hand off her shoulder. 'I didn't think you were so naïve. They don't make girls like that any more. I thought you above everyone would have known that.'

For a moment she thought he would strike her, but after a second he got himself under control, the broad shoulders relaxed and he gave a short mirthless laugh. 'Of course.' He raked his fingers through the long dark hair. 'Of course.' His eyes were blank now and his mouth had tightened into a thin gash. 'Only remember while you're my wife your . . . activities will have to be curtailed.'

'Really.' She adopted a slow drawl designed to annoy him, turning away at the same time. 'As to that I shall do as I choose but I promise you, I shall be discreet. And, of course, I expect the same from you. I don't want you to flaunt . . . ' She broke off, unwilling to let him know how much she resented his association with Freddie Galston.

'Go on,' he said silkily. 'You don't want me to flaunt . . . what, Bianca?'

'Your girl-friends,' she went on smoothly. 'If I'm to exercise restraint then I expect you to do the same.'

'I shall please myself.' He followed her along the short corridor and bending in front of her turned the handle of the door to the bedroom so that she could go in ahead of him. 'But then I always have shown discretion in that respect.' He stood in front of her in the centre of the bedroom and pulled from his pocket a folded newspaper. 'And I would like to re-emphasise just how much

I dislike being at the centre of this kind of rag.' He tossed it down on one of the twin beds.

Without wishing to, Bianca looked down, seeing that the tabloid was folded open at page three which was dominated by a series of pictures of Daniel. In each of them he was accompanied by a beautiful woman, at least three of whom Bianca knew had taken part in one of his programmes, and a headline screamed coyly of tomorrow's wedding.

'I see.' Amusement disguised the stab of anguish that the report caused her. 'And this is what you consider discretion?'

'No, it isn't. And that's why I've no intention of providing them with any further articles. You've had your little joke at what you thought was my expense.' He didn't have to tell her that he still considered she had been responsible for the leak of news about the wedding. 'Now that it has rebounded on you with a certain amount of violence,' the thought appeared to give him a little pleasure which he savoured before continuing, 'perhaps you will have learned your lesson.' His expression hardened. 'So long as we are married you will do as I say. Any stepping out of line will have fairly serious consequences. Do you understand what I mean?'

She refused to answer him but took up something he had said. 'So long as we are married,' she repeated coldly. 'Am I to be told exactly what you mean by that? It would help if I were to have some idea of just how long I'm to be required to pay the price of my brother-in-law's mistakes.' The thought that they were discussing divorce before they were even married struck her as so macabre as to bring tears to her eyes and in order to conceal them she turned away, dropping the newspaper on the floor as she did so.

'It shouldn't be too long.' He paused. 'Shall we say six months at the most. I think that should give time enough for all the ends to be sufficiently tied up. If at the end of that time I'm still not certain that I've got exactly what I want,' the gleam in the dark eyes was oddly disconcerting, 'then I shall give you notice. But, I hope not to hang on to you longer than is absolutely necessary. I can assure you that I value my freedom every bit as much as you do yours. Oh and,' the pause was so long that she knew he was underlining what he had to say, 'Lex didn't make any "mistakes". Not unless you consider being found out a mistake. He did exactly what he intended doing, subdividing his company, nominating his wife to the various boards where that appeared to be the most advantageous thing to do. It was all very carefully thought out, some people might call it devious, and it was most certainly dishonest, involving enormous sums of money. But none of it was a mistake, so don't let your imagination run away with you. Now,' his voice was grim, his eyes searing, 'let me have your doorkey.' The hand he held out brooked no refusal. 'I'll make another trip to your flat for the rest of your things and when you've got them put away I'll run you back.' He took the key she fished from the pocket of her waistcoat. 'Oh and,' casually he tossed the key into the air once or twice, each time catching it with a swift downward snatch of long brown fingers, 'in case I don't have the chance to speak to you again about the wedding,' his voice was full of contempt as he spoke that word, 'remember that I expect a star performance from you tomorrow. If you don't play your part properly I may just change my mind about Comyn International. So,' a step brought him close to her, and the hand holding the key fastened round the upper part of her arm making her long to cry out in pain, 'don't let me have second thoughts, Bianca. Not unless you decide you don't care whether your sister ends up in prison or not.' Then he turned and walked out of the flat.

Everyone agreed that it was the prettiest wedding they had ever seen. Elspeth was the first to spell out what the mirror had already told the bride. Elspeth, who had rushed back to town late on Friday just so Bianca wouldn't spend her last night of spinsterhood alone. She had meant well but Bianca's heart had sunk when she had first heard the door open and her friend calling a greeting from the hall. For the few hours of the wedding she thought she could just about maintain the pretence, but this evening as well . . . But in the end she had found Elspeth's cheerfulness and good sense a great relief from her own morbid thoughts.

And this morning her admiration was positively uplifting.

'You look so stunning that I'm almost changing my mind about a white wedding.' She adjusted the hem of Bianca's skirt and sat back on her heels admiringly. 'I wish it was Jim and me.'

'It'll be you and Jim before you know where you are.' Briefly Bianca forgot her own position was very far from that of the normal bride as she comforted her friend. Besides she hardly required her friend's assurances, her reflection was telling her what she wanted to know . . .

The pure silk suit in a most subtle shade of jade with large white spots was utterly simple but devastatingly chic. It had cost the earth when she had been in the mood to spend everything she had for this day. Pain twisted her stomach but she wrenched her mind away from what was intolerable. Under the jacket she wore a white crêpe-de-

chine tee-shirt which clung softly to her curves. Purely
to suit her hat, a tiny white felt one with a bunch of jade
flowers on the side and a black eye-veil, she had styled
her hair on the top of her head but leaving a gentle frame
of curling coppery strands about her face.

Her make-up was deceptively simple emphasising the
naturally honey tones of her skin, eyelids touched with a
colour that took up the jade of her suit, full mouth
outlined with a pinky-fawn gloss. She surveyed herself
with bleak complacency, deciding that Daniel would be
getting at least some value for his money.

'Now what else is there?' Elspeth busied herself making sure that nothing had been forgotten. 'You say that
your cases are safely stowed away in Daniel's car and
that he has your passport.'

'Yes.' Bianca turned away from the satisfaction of her
own reflection, reached for her new black handbag and
gloves which were lying on the chair beside the long
fleecy knitted overcoat. 'Yes, everything's under control. All we have to do is wait for Daniel to collect us.'

'Aren't you lucky!' Elspeth, usually so matter-of-fact,
showed some sign of emotion. 'Daniel to take care of
you for the rest of your life.'

'Yes, aren't I?' And she was glad that the sarcasm of
her comment was lost on Elspeth in the sudden ringing of
the doorbell.

Her heart turned over when she saw him. It was
impossible to think of anything but how devastating he
looked, she was even aware of how Elspeth, mad about
Jim as she might be, gave him a sighing glance before she
ostentatiously went out of the room so that they could be
alone together. He was wearing a dark suit, one that she
had never seen before and which looked absolutely new,
with the narrowest of red stripes. A white silk shirt and a

foulard tie patterned in red and grey, completed the outfit, and there was a matching red rose in his buttonhole.

His eyes were mocking as he bowed and kissed her cheek, going through all the proper motions for the benefit of Elspeth who was rattling things in the kitchen but who might overhear. 'You look beautiful, my sweet.' How she hated those words as a form of endearment. 'I'm a very lucky man,' he said insincerely.

'But I,' there were daggers in her glance, 'think I'm the one who has all the luck.'

He took her left hand, still looking deep into her eyes with that curious probing yet cynical expression, raised it to his lips and kissed it briefly, then she felt something being slipped on to her finger. The brilliance of the diamonds caught the light, and the square-cut emerald gleamed extravagantly so that Elspeth coming back into the sitting-room gasped when she saw the ring on Bianca's finger.

'It's been such a rush,' Daniel explained. 'Since we decided to get married I've scarcely seen Bianca. But I did want her to have my engagement ring on her finger before the knot was finally tied.'

'Gosh.' There was a trace of envy in Elspeth's admiration. 'What I wouldn't do for a ring like that.'

'You're too late telling me that,' Daniel joked. 'Now if I had known earlier . . .'

'How did you know that emeralds were Bianca's favourite stone? Did she drop a hint?'

'Let's say I knew instinctively. We hadn't mentioned the subject of an engagement ring but I thought with her colouring emeralds would be a safe bet. I got it when I was in Luxemburg.'

'I don't know about you two.' Elspeth bustled about

happily collecting her things. 'You seem happy to do everything the wrong way and yet it turns out for the best. When she told me she was going to be married in green, I nearly died. Then, you and she going *together* to the wedding. I would never have the nerve to break so many conventions.'

'And we're taking you along with us. Is that also a taboo?' Daniel smiled down at her disarmingly as he caught hold of her arm. 'And being late?' he queried in amusement. 'I hope you don't have any plans to keep us chatting here while the guests get frantic at the registrar's, Elspeth?' The smile he directed towards his fiancée was less amiable than the one he saved for Elspeth. 'You know they won't wait like a vicar might do, so if you're trying to waste time so that we can't get married, forget it. You see, my mind's made up. I *am* going to marry Bianca today. Nothing is going to stop me.' And with masterful charm he guided them both towards the door.

And much later that day when they were sitting close together yet a million miles apart in the first-class section of the aeroplane which was taking them on their honeymoon, Bianca sat twisting the emerald ring on her finger. Above it was the wedding ring which he had put there, three—no, four hours earlier and it was obvious that they were a matching pair. The chasing on the platinum wedding ring was the same as that on the engagement ring, but it wasn't that fact that was troubling her. At the back of her mind something was niggling away, some problem which didn't quite fit into the pattern as a whole. It had been with her all the time they had been driving to the registrar's office, she had almost forgotten it during the time it took for the short service to be performed, but when they had been at Claridge's for the luncheon it had nagged at the back of her mind through all the laughter, all the speeches which erroneously marked this out as an ordinary wedding.

Bianca sighed and turned her head so that she looked through the window on to a carpet of fleecy clouds, tinted pink in the sun's rays. Since they had come on board all pretence of normality had been abandoned. They were like a middle-aged couple who had nothing to say to each other any more, each behaving with perfect politeness but it was the politeness that existed between strangers. He hadn't even remembered that she felt nervous when taking off. That had really hurt her; tears had stung behind her closed eyelids and one or two had squeezed themselves free and trickled down her cheeks. But she had bitten her lip fiercely, enduring the stinging saltiness on her cheeks until she had eventually regained control.

When they were airborne and seatbelts were released, he had asked her if she would like to remove her hat, had watched sombrely while she unpinned it, and then he had laid it carefully on top of her already folded white coat. He had then sat down again and opened a paperback book, making it quite clear how he meant to pass the long hours of the journey.

She wondered how they were going to spend two weeks in the Seychelles. That was where they were going for the honeymoon, she had discovered. It might as well have been Blackpool or the Isle of Dogs for all she cared, but it would be warm there, that was one thing, so perhaps it would be possible to survive.

She moved her head and became aware of his hand lying on the arm of his seat. The book had fallen from his fingers, much as hers had done on that first flight, providing the opening shot in what had turned out to be such a dirty fight. If she moved her left hand the merest fraction their fingers would touch. It was strange how powerful the inclination was to do just that, in spite of everything. At the base of her spine nerves tingled, and no matter how much she tried to obliterate the recollection from her mind, she remembered just how tender, how sensitive those fingers could be against her skin.

She spread out her hand and the jewels blazed in the light. His gift to her. And hers to him? She thought of the small beautifully wrapped package at the bottom of her case, put there before Freddie Galston had turned her world upside-down. And now she didn't know if she could ever give him the beautiful gold cufflinks with his initials engraved on them. When she had bought them she had imagined slipping them into his shirt-cuffs while he was dressing, had thought that perhaps he would groan with frustration and would pull her close to him and that their plans to go down to dinner would have to be postponed while he . . .

Luxemburg. The thought came into her mind, sending all those tormenting visions fading into the background for the time being. She frowned. There had been some mention of Luxemburg but the significance of it still escaped her. Inadvertently, her hand brushed against his, sending all her senses jangling with perverse excitement. Bianca glanced up at Daniel as if it were his fault. But instead of being asleep as she expected him to be, after all she thought indignantly he had dropped his book and he had been breathing very evenly, he was watching her through narrowed eyes. And his expression was far from reassuring.

CHAPTER EIGHT

THE hotel was the last word in luxury. Bianca stood in the sitting-room of the suite listening while Daniel supervised the placing of their cases on the rack in the hall, heard the murmur of voices, the clink of coins, the departure of the porter. It was an effort for her to smile her appreciation at the dark-skinned maid who had bustled into the flat ahead of them, throwing back the windows and sun shades that led on to a large balcony, then going into the bedroom where presumably she turned down the covers. Bianca didn't follow her to check that.

Instead she walked, with a listless, fatigued gait across to the verandah, enjoying the warm breeze on her face as she leaned on to the rail. Beneath her and to the left was a huge swimming pool, irregularly shaped, softly lit. The shallow children's end was connected to the main part by an isthmus surmounted by a short humpbacked bridge. The area about the pool was paved with pale-coloured marble slabs with enormous troughs filled with exotic looking flowers, and the concealed lighting floodlit the blue water.

The hotel was perched above a bay and she could hear the insistent crash of waves on the beach; the sea which glittered in the light from a million stars she supposed must be the Indian Ocean. If he had shown any inclination to discuss their destination on the journey she would have been able to have all her questions answered. She sighed, slipped the jacket from her shoulders so that the

138

touch of the tropic air caressed her skin, then started guiltily as a shape appeared at her elbow.

She turned round to face him, blushing when she saw his eyes move over the clinging silk of her shirt, displeased that his expression showed neither approval nor disapproval.

'They're sending up some food. The restaurant is closed now.'

'Of course.' She dragged her eyes from his and looked with feigned interest towards the view. 'What time is it?'

'Local time, five a.m. We've lost a few hours during the flight. Ah,' there was a note of relief in his voice when a bustle in the hall and the rattle of crockery signalled the arrival of the food, 'here it is.'

The light meal consisting of a mild curry of eggs and seafood followed by fruit was eaten more or less in silence, during which Bianca felt her resentment and agitation rise to an absolute crescendo. When she had finished she got up from the comfortable chair, one of several grouped round a glass-topped table, steeling herself to say what she decided must be made clear from the beginning. 'I imagine I'm to have the bedroom,' she waved a hand towards the long sofa drawn up against the inside wall, 'the settee looks totally comfortable.'

'Yes, it does.' He stood up too, tossing off the last drop of wine in his glass. Hers remained where she had left it, having conspicuously refused to allow a drop to pass her lips. He said no more but continued to survey her with that mixture of contempt and anger which she supposed she would have to get used to. Confused by this as much as by the leashed anger she sensed in him she walked away towards the bathroom, collecting her overnight things en route.

The shower was warm and relaxing and by the time

she was ready for bed she was suddenly conscious of how
exhausted she felt. On her way to the bedroom she
murmured an ungracious goodnight to Daniel who had
piled the remains of their supper on the trolley and
wheeled it into the hall, but she got no reply which did
not surprise her.

The bedroom was a dream location for a honeymoon
she thought sourly as she chose the bed furthest from the
door, which she closed with a firmness she hoped would
not be wasted on her husband. Although they were twin
beds, each was as large as a double and the smooth
cotton sheets were welcoming as she slid her legs down
and pulled the covers up to her waist. She had just laid
her face against the cool pillow when the door was
thrown open with as much firmness as she had shown in
its closing. The eyes which had been drooping with
weariness shot open and Bianca sprang to a sitting
position.

Indignation drove off almost immediately that first
little throb of excited fear, especially when she saw
Daniel survey her with a cool unwinking expression as
he began to undo the buttons of his shirt.

'What do you think you're doing?' she gasped.

'What does it look like?' Idly he pulled the shirt from
the band of his trousers, then paused while he undid the
links fastening his cuffs. 'I'm getting ready for bed.'

'But—' the sight of that brown powerful chest sprinkled
with dark hair was not conducive to clear thinking,
'—you said you would sleep in the other room.'

'Correction.' He threw the shirt away from him in a
gesture of controlled ferocity. 'That was what you said.'
He lowered himself on to the side of the other bed and
without taking his eyes from her, kicked off the dark
slip-on shoes. 'I made a point of not agreeing with you.'

'How dare you!' If it wasn't that she had left her negligee on the foot of *his* bed, she would have flounced out of the room and acted the martyr by taking the settee in the sitting-room herself. Only, the nightdress she was wearing was scarcely decent and even sitting up like this, with her top half covered with one or two wisps of lace and ribbon, it might give him the idea that . . . Colour flooded her face as she saw the cynical, approving way in which he allowed his eyes to linger about her tumbled hair and bare skin, and she realised that the same thought must have occurred to him as well.

'You— You—' She snatched the sheet up and held it under her chin, then gasped as he began to undo the waistband of his trousers. She collapsed on to her pillow, averting her face and trying to prevent the tears of vexation squeezing from her closed eyes.

'Yes, I know. Words fail you,' he said drily and then she heard the sound of his bare feet coming across the polished wood floor, round the end of her bed, finally stopping somewhere very close, so close that the faint lingering scent of his cologne came disturbingly to her nostrils. For what seemed a long time he stood there, and she lay with fiercely beating pulses, willing him to go away, afraid to open her eyes until she was certain that he had done so.

'You know, for a woman of your experience you're a great prude, Bianca. You needn't be, you know, for I'm quite decent.'

'Really.' She snapped her eyes open at him, lying back on her pillows so that he should not mistake her animosity, but she could not avoid seeing he had wrapped a small blue towel about his waist. 'I still would prefer it if we could have separate rooms.'

'Look,' the slight easing of his manner which had been

apparent when he last spoke, disappeared, 'I'm not much interested in how *you* feel right at the moment. *I'm* exhausted, and the only concession I'm prepared to make is that I don't mind sharing a room with you. I assure you that you're quite safe.' His eyes drifted over her bare shoulders again but this time she wouldn't give him the satisfaction of running for cover. 'No matter how inviting you *think* you are. So long as you don't snore, I think I'll manage to put up with the situation.' He turned and walked away to the door, quite oblivious of the pillow which Bianca heaved after him. Then, when the water was gushing from the bathroom shower and she felt it was safe to do so, she got up and reclaimed the pillow. And when he came back, she lay perfectly still in her bed, pretending sleep.

When she woke the room was deliciously warm and shady, net curtains drifted gently into the room on the faintest of breezes while the sunshade over the verandah protected the room from the brilliance of the sun. Bianca lay for a moment unable to imagine where she was and then recollection hit her. On the pillow her head turned, eyelids opened lazily then flicked wide when she realised that the bed across from hers was empty, the clothes turned back as if he had gone carefully. She yawned, then lay for a time, recollections stealing into and out of her mind as the events of the past few days returned to haunt her. If only . . . If only she hadn't known, then she and Daniel could have been on a real honeymoon. Her mouth softened, there was a curious stirring within her until she sat up and swung her legs out of bed in determination.

Don't be an idiot, she told herself. His plan was to leave you at the altar. Or at least in the registrar's. That, she thought with a shiver as she pulled the nightdress

over her head, would have been so much worse. Then
she was astonished at herself—how could anything be
worse than the situation they were in now?

She had showered and dressed in a bikini under a light
cotton kanga when the maid of the previous night
brought in a breakfast tray which she placed on the table
out on the balcony.

Bianca had eaten the fruit and was drinking her
second cup of coffee when she saw Daniel, dressed only
in swimming trunks, coming along a path which
appeared to wind up from the beach. In one hand he was
holding a pair of flippers and she saw the flash of white
teeth as he smiled at the girl who was walking just a step
behind him.

There was rage in his wife's heart, so potent that she
could scarcely swallow the featherlight roll she had
buttered, as she watched the pair come closer to the area
of the pool, apparently in no hurry, and stand there for a
long time, giving the impression that they were enjoying
a mild flirtation. Daniel raised one bare foot on to a low
wall, and leaned his elbow on his knee as if he had all the
time in the world, while the girl sank on to the wall,
getting up rather quickly as if she had found it too hot
and then brushing sand from her rump in a blatantly
provocative way. She saw them both laugh again then
Daniel straightened, offered the flippers to the girl who
put out a hand without actually taking them from him.
Bianca was too far away to be able to see if their fingers
were touching, but . . . Again she saw the flash of teeth as
they smiled at each other, in fact she heard the deep
laugh which served to remind her of the bitter-sweet past
as at last the couple prepared to part. Daniel turned in
the direction of the hotel whereas the girl seemed about
to take a path among some palm trees which might have

led to an annex of the hotel. Above the treetops a few
thatched rooftops could just be discerned. Bianca had
the impression that his eyes immediately found her
figure on the balcony and that was what made him turn
back to the girl. They stood close together for a few
seconds and then he came strolling back towards the
main building.

When he reached their suite Bianca had perched her
sunglasses on her nose and had a straw bag containing all
her bits and pieces ready. He leaned against the door
giving her time to become very aware of him, from the
white towel looped round his neck, exaggerating the
colour of his skin, to the powerful bare legs covered with
a fuzz of dark hair. He removed his dark glasses as if he
wished to study her then walked slowly into the centre of
the room.

'Did you sleep well?'

Unable to tolerate the look in his eyes, she turned
away from him, speaking with the glibness she would
have used to a stranger. 'Very well.' Facing her reflection she fiddled with one or two strands of hair which had
escaped from the scarf stitched inside her wide straw hat.
'And you?'

'Fine.' His eyebrows were drawn together in a swift
frown and he turned away impatiently. 'You got breakfast?' His glance towards the remnants on the balcony
gave the answer so she didn't trouble to speak. 'I
was awake early and you were sleeping soundly so
that I didn't feel like disturbing you. Now I think I'll
go and have a shower.' He turned in the direction of
the bathroom. 'Are you going to the beach or to the
pool?'

'I—I haven't decided.' Suddenly she felt lonely and
neglected.

'Well the beach is only fifty yards away but there are fairly big breakers at the moment. I think I'd rather you waited till I can come with you.'

'I'm not a child you know.' It gave her a perverse pleasure to contradict. 'And I can swim.'

'I'm sure you can, Bianca.' His gentleness was disconcerting as was the sudden prick of tears at her eyes, tears which fortunately the dark glass did much to conceal. 'All I'm saying is, stay by the pool till I come down. If you want to go down to the beach, then we can go together.' His grin was sudden and even more disconcerting than his gentleness had been. 'After all,' he walked into the bathroom and spoke above the swish of the shower, 'I *could* be in a very awkward position if a freak wave came and carried you out to sea.'

Bianca walked out of the suite, banging the door behind her, and imagined as she walked down the sweeping marble staircase that she could hear his mocking laughter following her.

But she did decide to stay beside the pool, partly because it was so pleasant there with loungers scattered over the grass and thatched umbrellas offering plenty of shade, and partly because she made a friend in the first moment when a small girl rushing across the wet tiles to the pool slipped, cannoned into Bianca and almost knocked her down.

'Be careful, Charlotte,' the mother remonstrated while the child flew on paying no attention. 'I'm sorry about that.' The young woman, recumbent on one of the chairs, smiled apologetically.

'That's all right.' Bianca paused and looked back to where Charlotte was splashing along with some other children in the shallow end of the pool. 'She seems to be enjoying herself anyway.'

'Oh, we all are.' The woman stretched luxuriously. 'It would be hard not to in a place like this.' Invitingly she hooked another chair with a bare foot, pulling it towards her. 'Borrow Dave's seat for a bit. He's taken Joey down to the sea.' She waited till Bianca sank down on to the edge of the lounger, 'You just arrived?'

'Yes. Late last night.'

'That's the only drawback,' she sighed. 'Coming in at three in the morning, it's no good with kids. Are you on your own?' Curiously she glanced at Bianca's left hand where the brand-new wedding ring was standing out like a cattle brand.

'No,' she answered in what she hoped was a careless tone. 'I'm with my husband.' It was the very first time she had acknowledged it and she felt a slow remorseless wave of colour sweep over her features. But luckily at that moment a man and boy came jogging across the grass and Bianca found. herself being introduced to Dave and Joey.

'And I'm Helen Brown.' She paused a moment while she applied some sun-filter cream to her son's shoulders. 'Oh, don't go.' She glanced up as Bianca rather awkwardly got up from the seat. 'Dave can pull over another one. Hello—' Her voice drifted away as she concentrated on the figure coming towards them across the grass. 'Who . . . is this?'

A moment later Daniel, dressed in navy shorts and white open-necked shirt, was smiling down into Bianca's face with every appearance of affection; he draped one arm about her shoulder while the other hand solicitously removed the bag from her hand. Bianca's heart was throbbing uncomfortably as she completed a few sketchy introductions then she subsided into the chair again as the three males began to push a ball back and forth to each other across the grass.

'So that's your husband, Bianca?' Helen seemed to find it a fascinating thought, one that kept her eyes riveted on Daniel's tall lean figure as he became more absorbed in the football game. 'I have the feeling I've seen him somewhere . . .'

It was time to change the subject. 'Have you much longer? On holiday, I mean?'

'What? Oh no. We go home the day after tomorrow. Back to cold old England.' She shivered. 'The holiday of a lifetime and now it's nearly over. But it's been idyllic.' She lay back on her chair with her eyes closed. 'I'm only sorry . . . My parents wanted to come, too, but they left it too late.'

'Oh?' Bianca was only half listening, her eyes were watching Daniel in this totally unfamiliar scene, apparently absorbed in a game with a child. Her heart bounded as she heard him shout a warning to Joey who just managed to return his father's awkward shot, then grinned in conspiratorial triumph at Daniel who winked back at him.

'Yes. We booked up some time ago but Dad couldn't arrange his leave until the last minute. Then of course the holiday was filled up.'

'Oh.' Bianca still was listening only mechanically. 'I thought with the recession there would be plenty of vacancies.'

'Apparently not. At least, not at the more expensive end of the market.'

'Oh?' Bianca lost all interest in the difficulties of the tour industry.

'Yes, if they had gone a day or two sooner they might have got in.' She yawned wearily. 'But Dad just got his dates fixed a fortnight ago. Oh, I think I'll have to go and have some coffee.' She sat up and began rummaging in her bag. 'Would you like one?'

'No.' Something at the back of her mind was confused, as it had been the previous night. 'No, thank you. I've just had breakfast.' As she spoke Daniel came back and threw himself on to the ground beside her, the dark eyes behind smoked glass held hers.

'Well, you said you'd like to go to the beach, darling.' The endearment rolled off his tongue as if he meant it and she decided that for the moment she would play along with him.

'All right.' Eyes flashed towards him while her mouth smiled. 'Let's go, shall we . . . darling.'

'Now that,' he kept his arm about her shoulders till they reached the corner where they were hidden from the Brown's view when he allowed it to drop to his side, 'seemed almost effortless on your part.'

'Thank you,' she said drily but with a hint of amusement which she didn't trouble to conceal. Besides it was too hot and too lyrically beautiful in this corner of the world to keep up the heat of animosity. And there was something else. When she had a moment to herself she would try to work things out, but now was not the moment because they emerged quite suddenly from the path that had wound through the tall palms, and there before them, in all its raging power and beauty, the Indian Ocean tossed itself against a sickle of pale sand, densely fringed with coconut palms.

'Oh, Daniel.' She spoke his name softly, without even noticing that she was doing so. 'It's heavenly.' There was a surge of something incomprehensible in her throat and she turned to him.

But he had stepped away, standing with legs apart, hands on hips and staring out to where two surfers were hurtling towards the beach on the crest of a huge wave. Bianca, following the direction of his interest, held her breath as one of them, she could see both were female, lost her balance, disappeared and reappeared several times under the rollers before at last being tossed in an untidy heap on the beach. She got up at once, rushed after her surf board, caught it and joined her companion who was walking slowly up the beach.

Then she caught sight of the two figures watching from the shade of the trees and an arm was raised towards Daniel in a friendly gesture, tossing back the streaming fair hair from her forehead.

'Daniel.' She had an intriguing accent, speaking his name at the back of her throat like a caress. 'Have you come to join us?' With total assurance she came striding across to them, her brilliantly blue eyes taking in Bianca in a swift appraisal before turning the battery of her smile on the man.

Daniel shook his head and grinned. 'No. Not this time I'm afraid, Martine.'

'Oh, pity.' She pouted and walked on without pausing. 'Another time perhaps,' she called over her shoulder. And Bianca looked with dislike at the girl whom she had instantly recognised as the one Daniel had been speaking to earlier. The one he had obviously picked up on the beach before he had been married even twenty-four hours. She threw herself down on the warm sand and turned deliberately away from him.

But it was impossible to sulk for long. After all, she told herself, why should she care if the man she was married to was an inveterate womaniser? He meant nothing to her so why not forget what had happened and just enjoy the holiday.

And that admonition seemed effective because by the time she and Daniel strolled up for a late lunch at the poolside restaurant they were at least speaking to each other. They exchanged a few words with Joey Brown who pushed past them carrying a brimming glass of Coca-Cola and Daniel managed to get into conversation with a middle-aged German couple at the next table to the one they had chosen.

Whether it was the effects of the wine, the sun or simply jet lag Bianca found that she could hardly keep her eyes open at the end of the meal and was glad when Daniel's steps led them towards the staircase and up to their suite. She had a quick shower and when she went into the bedroom wrapped again in her kanga, tucked sarong-style under her arms she saw that Daniel was lying on his back on his bed, reading the paperback book which had kept him so occupied on the journey the previous day.

'All right?' he asked lazily without seeming to take his eyes from the book.

'Mmm.' She felt ridiculously self-conscious. Her heart was hammering against her ribs and she made a note to resist the temptations of wine at least during lunch after this. It always had a distinctly disturbing effect on her. And Daniel, lounging so close to her, did nothing to help. 'I'm so—' A hiccup spoiled the effect of cool sophistication she would have liked to promote. 'so sleepy.'

'Mmm.' Clearly he was hardly listening to what she was saying and didn't notice her sour glance as he turned a page, 'It's the sun.'

Without further conversation Bianca lay down, slipping her legs beneath the sheets. But sleep which had been so infinitely desirable moments before was all at once elusive. She lay, listening to the occasional flick as Daniel turned a page of his book, then after a long time she heard his weight move on the bed, his breathing become deeper, more even and a soft swish as the book dropped from his fingers on to the floor.

Gently, determined not to make the slightest sound, she turned in the bed, keeping her eyes closed so if he were still awake he might imagine she was moving in her sleep. For a time she continued to lie feigning sleep before gathering courage to open her eyes the merest slit. Then she saw his recumbent figure, arm sagging down towards the floor, his paperback book a few inches from his relaxed fingers and she opened her eyes fully so that she could study him.

The chest was rising and falling deeply, the movement was clear even under the sheet which was half pulled across to cover him. His head had fallen to one side and there was a frown on his face as if even in sleep he could not entirely escape from whatever was causing concern. Bianca, suddenly aware of the pain in the region of her heart, allowed a tiny protesting moan to escape her lips then with an impetuous gesture she wrenched her head round on the pillow so that she was no longer tormented by the sight of him.

Torment, that was a good description of how she was feeling. Ferociously she bit her lip to stop tears coming. And yet why should it be like that if she disliked him as much as she had promised herself she did. But no sooner had the idea come into her mind than she was filled with all the warm melting feelings she had known in those days when she had been preparing for her wedding; that urgent physical longing which had impelled her towards such a hasty marriage. And then she recognised what she had known subconsciously since the very beginning. She didn't hate him. She couldn't possibly hate him. Not while she loved him as she did.

All that pretence of a sacrifice for Cindy was just so much stuff and nonsense. There was only one reason why she was here at this moment, in this situation and with this man. And quite simply that was because she wanted to be with him. Always.

The acknowledgement seemed to bring her a little relief, there was an easing of the pain deep inside her and at last she fell asleep.

CHAPTER NINE

THEY hadn't realised that this was the weekly gala night in the hotel when after dinner there was a short cabaret followed by a dance. As she was getting ready, Bianca felt a surge of hope rising inside her like some irrepressible fermentation and that might have been the reason for her choosing the cream dress.

It was daring, quite unlike anything she had ever worn before. When she pulled it over her head when she was in the privacy of the bedroom, she twisted and turned to her reflection wondering if perhaps she had gone a bit too far in deciding to buy it. Certainly when she had tried it on in the fitting-room of the famous London store it hadn't seemed quite so . . .

A knock at the door took her whirling away from the mirror and when Daniel came into the room she was casually fixing her earrings, hoping that he would make no comment. He didn't, merely picked up a handkerchief from the wardrobe shelf and retreated to the sitting-room where he was waiting for her, giving no sign that his eyes had even glanced in her direction.

Almost fearfully Bianca returned to the long mirror, noticing with a gasp how the dress with its gorgeous clinging material seemed to fit her like a second skin. Certainly no one would be under any misapprehension that she was wearing anything under it. She even wondered, putting a hand to the full swell of her breast, if the material was entirely opaque, there were one or two suggestive shadows . . .

The halter neckline showed off shoulders that were beautifully smooth and even. In the hours since they arrived the colour of her skin had deepened so that it glowed against the warm contrasting shade. The skirt was as clinging as the bodice but it was slit to the thigh at one side so that movement was not hindered. It made her feel sexy and alluring, so in a wave of abandon she decided there was no way she would change.

She wore her hair loose, thick and coppery like a mane falling to her shoulders. With her left hand she touched its silky waves, feeling a thrill as the emerald and diamond ring caught fire from the light. In her ears she was wearing long drops, cheap glittery green glass but wonderfully effective even if no one would mistake them for gems. Feeling irrationally cheered, she picked up her small evening purse and walked with what confidence she could summon into the sitting-room.

Daniel spared her a glance as he stood up, his eyes lingering for a few moments on the form-hugging dress, but Bianca had her face averted and he said nothing about her appearance. But if her husband had shown no interest in how she looked she was sure he must have seen the admiring eyes that slid in her direction as they were led through the dining-room to a table close to the enormous windows, thrown back to the softness of the tropical darkness and which overlooked the swimming pool.

Now, of course, it was still and empty, merely a smooth blue surface on which still palm trees were reflected, as cool and clear as aquamarine crystal. Bianca sat gazing out on it while Daniel was busy with the waiter, finding it a peaceful solace for her tattered emotions.

Daniel leaned on the table and smiled across at her,

the first natural reaction since all the trouble started between them, and one which confirmed all those conclusions she had reached a few hours earlier. How could she have been so foolish as to pretend he meant little to her. To hide her feelings she looked down at the pink linen tablecloth, touched the spray of white stephanotis tucked inside the table napkin.

'Pretty,' she said, but she was hoping he would notice, too, how pretty her hands looked with the pink-tinted finger-nails and the new rings. When she glanced up at him through the fringe of long lashes he was looking to one side and she saw his attention had been attracted by the elderly German couple whom they had met earlier in the day. She smiled at the wife but used most of the time to take in the details of Daniel's appearance.

In common with most of the men, he was jacketless but the dazzling white shirt and pale slacks seemed only to emphasise his dark virility. The slight formality of a silk tie in shades of brown and fawn suited him and she had an overwhelming impulse to put out a hand to smooth down a strand of hair which had sprung up after his shower. But, luckily, he looked round, caught her eyes and she did nothing.

The meal was a delicious combination of European and Oriental food: the first course a brilliant mélange of pineapple and prawns, then Bianca ate pork flavoured with ginger and coconut while Daniel chose a stir-fried chicken dish. With this they drank a chilled white wine which Bianca, remembering her earlier reaction, sipped very slowly so that one glass lasted throughout the meal. Dessert turned out to be the eternal crème caramel or something that looked like a jam tart which caused them both a fit of the giggles, and instead they decided on fruit to finish. Afterwards they wandered through to the large reception area where they could drink coffee and wait for the cabaret to begin.

When they had risen from the table Bianca had been oblivious of everything except the touch of Daniel's hand on her elbow, and the fact that it had been dropped as soon as the niceties would allow had done nothing to still her surging feelings, nor to dampen her wildly soaring hopes.

Their silence was companionable enough and she was grateful that at least the cruel abrasiveness between them had mellowed. Even if it was the wine and the atmosphere which caused the easing, that at least was something. They sat in the dimness of the salon, lit here and there by soft coloured lights shaded by huge sea urchin and conch shells, listening to the throbbing music from a steel band.

Much of the music was amended pop but the locals had thrown over it an air that made it not inconsistent with their tropical surroundings, and nothing jarred. There was a show by a group of speciality dancers who owed more than a little to flamenco, but the clicking came from fingers rather than castanets and finally a young man sang what appeared to be a tale of forlorn love and revenge while strumming wildly on a mandola. Bianca found that she was quite happy just to sit and simply absorb it all. But at the same time she was very much aware of the effect this sensuous onslaught of sight and sound was having on her feelings. Was it possible that Daniel was as aware of her as she was of him? But of course that was asking the impossible.

During the period of the short cabaret there had been much coming and going and by the time it was over and the moment had come for dancing the room was quite full and buzzing with voices in every language. Daniel told her that while many of the guests were residents from the hotel he suspected that still more came from the blocks of self-service apartments farther along the beach towards the village.

And some of them were certainly noisy she decided as she and Daniel walked round the room towards the bar.

'What would you like, Bianca?' The raking glance from his dark eyes gave her a shock so that she stammered, blushed and screened her eyes with her long lashes.

'Oh . . . something long and cool. Coca-Cola, perhaps.'

'Could I recommend a Mahé shandy if you don't want anything alcoholic? It has lots of lime and ice topped up with lemonade and a dash of bitters.'

'That sounds lovely.' And when he turned away her eyes followed the tall figure to the bar before her attention was diverted by some jostling from a small group who were making their way through to the bar. There were six of them, three young men and three girls and they were talking loudly in German, laughing and obviously enjoying themselves. One of the men smiled invitingly at Bianca who resented his lingering glance over her figure and turned away with distaste.

Moments later Daniel was back with her drink and she turned to him in relief which showed in the blatant way her eyes sought his over the rim of her glass. But she found that her husband had apparently noticed someone more interesting than his twenty-four-hour wife and she turned to find out the reason for the raised glass salute to someone behind her.

Of course, she thought angrily, and wondered why she had not recognised one of the women who had just passed. It was the girl he had been with on the beach this morning, the one he had called Martine. She swung back but not before she had seen the girl raise a hand in greeting and begin to walk towards them.

'Daniel.' Her voice was as deep and throbbing as she had first thought, a strange voice coming from this tall girl with a figure as slim as a model's. Tonight she was wearing a shift dress in fiery orange and her sun-drenched blonde hair reached almost to her waist, hair which contrasted strongly, weirdly almost, with her deeply bronzed skin.

'Martine!' Daniel didn't trouble to hide his pleasure at the girl's approach, he might even have been relieved that someone else had joined them. 'It's nice to see you.'

'Well,' the blue eyes slid swiftly towards Bianca and apparently dismissed her easily, 'I did promise I would see you, did I not?'

'This is Bianca.' It was very noticeable that he did not explain their relationship thought Bianca resentfully as she gave the girl the briefest of greetings.

'May I present my friends to you?'

'Of course.' Daniel gestured towards a large table which had just been vacated. 'Let's sit there, shall we?' And a few moments later Bianca found herself sitting beside the young man who had been eyeing her so blatantly seconds before.

And her first thought was that perhaps she had mis-judged him. Wolfgang, she felt like laughing when he told her his name but he insisted that all his friends, and, he hoped, looking deeply into her eyes, she would do the same, called him Wolfie. He didn't look a bit wolfish no matter how he had behaved earlier, more like a cuddly, slighty tubby Teddy bear and she agreed she would use the same name as all his friends.

'That is *gut*.' He returned to his large glass of beer and

raised it to his lips, but without taking his slightly protuberant blue eyes from her face.

It was a blow to Bianca when, still smiling after the brief conversation with Wolfie, she turned round and found that Daniel and Martine had disappeared from sight. But not completely she saw as she watched them circle the dance floor in time to the slightly jerky waltz that was being played.

Not that there was anything jerky about their display. They were moving smoothly together—together being the most obvious part of the operation. Martine had linked her hands about Daniel's neck, that was common enough Bianca thought because almost every other couple on the floor had adopted the same style, and where else could his hands go but to circle his partner's waist? She was smiling up at him and he was looking down at her, the cat about to gobble up the cream. Jealousy was like a sword in her breast.

'You would like to dance, Bianca?'

'Thank you, Wolfie.' No one would have guessed how she was feeling as she walked on to the floor and turned holding out her hands to him. And no one would have guessed how uncomfortable she felt in his possessive grasp being pressed too close to his rotund stomach and with his excited breath in her ear.

Not even Daniel could have had any idea how she felt, especially as she failed to respond to his raised amused eyebrow as they danced past each other. For the next half hour she was the life and soul of the party, surprising herself and surprising even Daniel. Once or twice she saw him frown reprovingly in her direction but she gave the impression that she was having the time of her life and she was willing to dance with anyone who asked her. Everyone except her husband, of course. She made sure that he got that message from the way she ignored him completely while he danced with Martine and Karen and the one Bianca called Brunhild despite the fact that she had been introduced as Frieda.

In between times she found that her glass of Mahé shandy had been replaced twice, each time tasting slightly different although Wolfie and one of the other Germans who had brought them from the bar insisted that she was imagining things. By the time she got up to dance with Dave Brown who came across to her from one of the adjoining tables she was feeling abandoned in more ways than one and Daniel's disapproving expression only goaded her into a wild exhibition of the cha-cha-cha which would have made her blush normally.

'Thank you, Dave.' She leaned against him for a moment when the music ended, hoping that the room would stop going round before she had to go back to the table.

'I didn't know I could dance like that.' He grinned down at her. 'Tomorrow night when I'm back in London it will all seem like a dream.'

'Tomorrow? I forgot—maybe I'll see you before you go.' And she waved a hand as he turned away from her.

From the corner of her eye, Bianca saw how Daniel was pushing back his chair and fearing that he was coming with the intention of hustling her upstairs she looked round in desperation, catching hold of Wolfie in relief as he appeared in front of her. At once they drifted away, roughly in time with the smoochy tune that had replaced the vibrant sound of the Latin-American music. Smiling up into Wolfie's face she had a clear view of Daniel being intercepted by Martine who was clearly suggesting that they dance.

But as he stepped on to the floor with the girl it was

obvious that Daniel was far from happy and it was a moment or two before he smiled down into the German girl's face. Martine was, thought Bianca numbly as she missed a beat, giving Wolfie the excuse to hold her even closer, more protectively, like most of those girls you see on American television series, the ones who are always coming out of the ocean with surf boards, lithe and supple as prancing tigers, all sun-browned skin, sunbleached hair and large white teeth. Like tombstones, she decided, subduing a hysterical desire to laugh. If that was what Daniel liked . . .

Suddenly she felt her skin prickle with heat, nausea rose inside her making her gasp and turn towards the wide open doors.

'I'm feeling a bit giddy.'

'Of course, *liebchen.*' He really was kind. Considerate. As if it was a pleasure looking after her when she was feeling like this. 'Soon the fresh air will make you so much better.' He breathed the words against her cheek as he led her from the salon straight out on to the terrace. For a few moments they continued to dance in time to the music while he looked down at her. 'See, you are better already.' And with an arm supporting her he began to take her slowly round the side of the pool, away from the hotel, towards the path that led down towards the beach.

The fresh evening air did seem to give some relief after the heat and noise of the dance and Bianca felt the giddiness abating slightly although the sickness was still attacking her in waves. She remembered the seafood dish which she had eaten so greedily at dinner. It had tasted wonderful, that mixture of pineapple and prawns and yet the very thought of it now . . . With a positive effort she wrenched her mind away from it. You were always warned to be careful of what you ate when you came to the tropics . . .

'Shall we walk slowly down to the beach, *liebchen?* Then perhaps you will feel very much better.'

'No.' His voice so close to her reminded Bianca that his hands were linked about her waist as if that was where they had every right to be and from there it was just a step to noticing how hot and clammy his hands were, she could feel their warmth and dampness through her dress. 'No, thank you, Wolfie.' She tried to pull away from him, putting up her hands to her hair at the same time. 'I'm all right now. So maybe we'd better go back.'

But her movements had the opposite effect from the one she had planned because his hands slipped lower, imprisoning the curves of her hips and pulling her close to his body. At the same time his breathing seemed to increase, he became more excited and she found herself clasped in a determined embrace, while his lips searched for hers. At once she turned her face away, loathing the thought of his mouth on hers, but this seemed to inflame him further and his mouth dropped to her throat.

'Stop it, Wolfie!' She hissed the words at him, for the first time coolly considering how the present situation would appear to Daniel if he should happen to witness it. The very thought made her shudder but also forced a calmness which might just help her to keep things under control. 'Stop it, Wolfie!' She pushed strongly against his chest. 'I want to go back to the dance.'

He murmured something in his own language, but his arms tightened about her and at the same time his fingers pulled at the back fastening which kept her halter neckline in position. As the bodice of her dress slipped down his impatient fingers dragged at it and he lowered his head to her now exposed breast.

'No! No!' As she pushed at him, Bianca for the first time in her life understood just how impotent a woman can be against a determined male. In spite of his appearance of faintly decadent self-indulgence, she was no match for him and he scarcely seemed to notice her hands hammering against his face and chest. 'Stop it, damn you! If you don't . . .' Her voice faded away on a gasp.

But he only laughed, a low basic sound which made her skin crawl with apprehension and even a tinge of fear. What was she doing here, alone with a man she didn't know and whom she had disliked from the first moment!

'*Ach, liebling.*' His voice was thick. '*Ich . . .*'

'Let me go.' A sob tore from her throat. 'You idiot! If you don't I'll . . .'

Just then some invisible force took hold of the heavy brutish form and he was slammed back against the trunk of a palm tree. In the semi-darkness he sprawled there like a stranded whale, dazed and obviously trying to think what had happened to him. There was something freakish about the scene, this romantic situation; faint music from the direction of the hotel, stars scattered extravagantly against a sky of dark blue velvet and herself here with this fat German. But Bianca had never felt less like laughing. Then suddenly to one side and slightly behind her something shadowy moved and she realised just who had come to protect her.

Or to humiliate her. Shaking hands began to attend to her disordered dress and she was glad of the darkness hiding her burning cheeks. But it offered little protection from the scorn and disdain in his expression.

'Go and wait for me at the hotel.' His voice whipped at her like a lash, and his eyes showed more contempt and anger for her than for her assailant. 'While I settle things here.'

'Daniel, I . . . You won't . . .' Hopeless to explain that right now her concern was for him, for his safety. The words she would have wanted to use escaped her at this moment, a moment she felt could never be properly explained to him.

'Do as I tell you.' There was something brutal in his reply, in the way he didn't even glance in her direction, but kept his eyes on the other man while he moved towards him.

Miserably, her high heels catching on an exposed root so that she stumbled, Bianca walked away from the two men, trying as she reached the circle of light about the pool to appear as if she were perfectly at ease, even nodding to an elderly couple who looked at her with curiosity as they walked from the hotel towards one of the annexes.

Behind her she could hear voices, one raised in protesting explanation, the other lower and much more controlled. Then she heard, or thought she did, something more explosive, that might have been a clenched fist encountering a chin. Bianca groaned, put her hands over her ears and ran round to the side door of the hotel.

The entrance was one much used during the day as it was a convenient short cut for those with small children who wanted to use the shallow part of the pool. At this time of night it was deserted and she skulked in the shadow of a huge coco-de-mer, terrified of being seen. All she wanted to do was to rush away somewhere so that she could hide herself until the scars of her humiliation had begun to heal. And yet she knew she dare not move from this spot until Daniel came back. Besides, there was a simple little thing like the doorkey which he had. She could of course go to the main desk and collect the passkey but that way she might just bump into some of the Germans. If she did she knew she would be sick on the spot.

Then quite suddenly Daniel was back beside her. Her startled glance could distinguish little from his appearance although he gave no sign of having been in a punch up. But his anger was as apparent as ever. It was there, in the glacial look he gave her, in the harsh strength of his fingers as they bit into the soft flesh of her upper arm. They were sure to leave hideous bruises where everyone could see them. A sob of self-pity rose in her throat at the very idea, but Daniel showed no sign of being moved by a sob or any other female weakness as he threw open the door of their suite and pushed her inside.

For a long time they stood in the hall, she facing him in a mood of defiance now, rubbing the spots where his fingers had been so merciless as he hustled her upstairs. And he of course was lying back against the door in the same accusing style he had used that day in his flat. In fact, Bianca thought with a touch of hysteria, there was an awful sense of déjà-vu about it for it had been much the same that day when he had thrust her inside Lex's study door. And even earlier, when he had come rampaging after her and Simon. She wanted to storm and shout at him only some deep instinct of preservation stopped her. Instead she poised herself for flight, and wished that she could get to bed. Tonight she didn't feel well enough to argue, with waves of sickness flowing over her again, and of course that was the moment he chose to attack, with a menacing step towards her as well as contemptuous words.

'How dared you flaunt yourself with a man like that!'

'A man like that?' Her voice hardly trembled but it was an effort to control the revulsion even the thought of Wolfie brought. She found a few strands of dignity and pulled them about her. 'A man like what? You did introduce me to him after all.'

'I do not expect each time you meet someone that I should have to pursue you to the bushes and prevent you from being raped.' His eyes lashed her. 'Or maybe you were less unwilling than you pretended.'

Bianca felt her face flame then a conflicting icy chill ran down her spine. 'Is that what you really think of me?' Her voice was very faint and distant.

'What am I to think when you dress like that?' There was something controlled but ferocious in the words he flung at her, dark angry eyes flicked from her face to her breast and back again.

'You saw the dress before you went downstairs. That was the time to protest about it if you thought it unsuitable.'

'*Then* I had no idea how you would behave.'

'And how did you behave?' The words were out before he had finished. She was determined to show him that his criticism was not going to be accepted with docile obedience, only the effect was slightly marred by the faint tremor in her voice. 'Was it all right for that woman to flaunt herself at you? Or you at her if it comes to that?' She had not meant to show him how much that had hurt her pride and bit her lip tightly, feeling tears trembling in her eyes.

'At least Martine and I didn't go off on our own at the first opportunity,' he sneered.

'Martine.' He wasn't the only one who could adopt that condescending, offensive tone. 'Martine. How wonderful it must be to be a man. Just,' she waved an expressive arm, 'just drift down to the beach on the first morning and you score.'

'Don't talk like that.' Eyes narrowed and he spoke through clenched teeth but Bianca, sensing she had caught him on the raw, wasn't in the mood to stop now.

'Mind you,' the room was beginning to move slowly round, 'she was a safe enough bet I would say. And talking about dresses . . .' she hiccuped, 'I don't think hers was so very discreet, with the front open down to her navel.'

'I told you not to talk like that.' He came close to her, seized her again by the arms and shook her. 'I meant it.' Abruptly he let her go again so that she had to put out a hand to steady herself. But he seemed not to notice that, only continued to look at her with that expression of loathing on his face. 'As far as Martine goes she's just somebody I bumped into when I was swimming this morning. That's all it was and the only reason I suggested joining them was, curiously enough,' he gave a quick humourless laugh, 'for your sake. I thought you might be glad of some company.'

'How kind of you.' Her smile was designed as a response to his. 'I don't know what you could possibly imagine I have in common with Martine and her friends.'

'From where I was sitting it seemed you had a great deal in common with them. The males at least.'

'I had to dance with someone,' she flashed angrily. 'I *do* like dancing. Or perhaps you had forgotten.'

'No.' He spoke soberly, sighing as he turned away and walked through to the sitting-room. Bianca, still not feeling quite steady, followed him and stood looking at his back while he picked up a pack of cigars. He lit one and only then raised his head to look at her. 'No, Bianca, I hadn't forgotten that.' The anger seemed suddenly to have ebbed away from him and he was looking at her contemplatively, with an air of sadness which she found so much more disturbing than his anger had been.

'Only,' he went on after a bit, 'I got the impression that you didn't want to dance with me. I decided that you preferred . . . the others.'

'How very convenient for you.' Another hiccup. 'That lets you out on all counts.'

'Oh, for heaven's sake!' Suddenly he was grinding out the cigar with a fierce pressure, as if he would have liked to pick up the heavy ashtray and toss it through the window, and possibly her after it.

'That's no answer to anything,' she spoke with a shade of unctuousness, 'but I can see you have no intention of justifying yourself.'

'Justifying myself.' He laughed briefly, then turned so he was speaking over his shoulder. 'Why should I justify myself?'

'Why should I?' Her control broke and she sobbed. 'Why should I have to?'

'Bianca.' He whirled round, catching her arms as she began to walk towards the bedroom. His normally mellow voice was harsh, his eyebrows were drawn together in a dark frown which would have halted her even if his strength had not.

'Yes.' She stood, determined to remain unmoved by the touch of his fingers against her skin, her face averted so she could study the backs of her hands, as if in them she might be able to find a solution to the unbearable present.

'I can't cope with this, Bianca.' With the abrupt release of his fingers something impelled her to turn round. 'I thought I could.' Now that she was studying him with more discernment, she saw etched on his face many of the signs of strain which she felt she herself was showing. A tiny piece of the hardness about her heart eased, she longed to go towards him, to put her head on to his chest and weep. Then perhaps he would lower his cheek on to her hair, his arms would close round her and he would murmur all the soothing little words which would dispel the unhappiness . . .

'I thought that maybe I could but I was wrong.' He shrugged and raked a hand through his hair, his grimace underlined the impression that he was trying to control some intense physical suffering.

And then the significance of his words probed through the barrier of her pain, probed like the flicking tongue of a serpent to reach the deeper more sensitive flesh, spitting poison straight at a nerve. She staggered with shock and anguish as she began to understand what he meant. He was telling her that their marriage must be immediately annulled, that he couldn't bear living with her for the six months he had originally suggested. Vaguely she thought of Cindy, but the wave of anxiety that might have been expected didn't come. Later it might but not now. All she could think of was herself. And Daniel. But somehow, probably because of the way her mind had been working, it was her sister's name that came to her lips.

'But Cindy. I can't . . . I can't bear it.' That statement expressed in a broken, totally defeated voice revealed all the anguish of the past days. 'I just can't bear it.'

'Don't!' It was a savage command ground out through clenched teeth and was followed by a bitter little laugh. 'Don't.' His eyes were on her face as he spoke but now the anguish she read in his expression was somehow more difficult to bear than all his harshness, all his anger

and contempt had been. 'You needn't worry, Bianca, I
have no intention of making Lex's business dealings
public. So you can go to bed and sleep with absolutely
nothing on your mind.' Another shrug, another little
laugh, uncertain, wholly unlike the Daniel Bohun she
thought she knew. 'I never had.'

'You—' Bianca felt as if the entire room was beginning to turn slowly round. 'What do you mean?'

'I mean, my dear Bianca,' he laughed and this time it
was an acknowledgement of his own foolishness, 'that I
knew all about Lex's business deals long before I met
you. To put it bluntly, he's a crook. But he's not the first
one I've met by a long chalk and I don't consider it my
business to act as watchdog for the Inland Revenue nor
do I set myself up as judge and jury as far as business
ethics are concerned. All I care is that from the time I
take over Comyn everything will be above board.'

'But I still . . .' Very gradually the room began to right
itself so that she was able to focus on his face again.

'You needn't worry. What I'm trying to tell you is that
there isn't much chance of Lex getting into trouble with
the Fraud Squad. At least if he does it won't be through
me, but of course I can't guarantee that someone else
might not drop him in it. Oh, and as far as Cindy is
concerned then you can forget it. There never was the
slightest chance of proceedings being taken against her.
She's involved, sure, but I know Lex well enough to
know where the blame actually lies.'

Bianca stared at him for a long time, unconscious that
her eyes were huge in her face, that her hair falling like a
cloud about her shoulders had taken on a rich glow from
the single lamp on a table by the door of the bedroom.
Daniel's eyes seemed unable to leave hers and the
expression she saw there was undermining rational

thought, making it impossible for her to begin to sort out . . .

'I hope through time you'll be able to forgive me, Bianca.' For a moment bleakness dismissed all warmth from his expression. 'It was a desperate situation and the remedy I chose was desperate, simply a wild gamble that didn't come off. But I'm not going to pretend that I have any regrets about trying it.' Abruptly he turned from her towards the window yet his back, the rigid way he was holding himself, gave the distinct impression that he was seeing nothing. 'Go to bed, Bianca,' he said harshly, 'before . . .' The rest of the sentence was clipped off angrily.

'Before . . . what, Daniel?' Her voice was slumbrous as if she were suddenly being whisked into a dream, a fairy tale where everything would turn out right on the last page. It was difficult to think what had caused such a sudden change, from bruising pain and disappointment to this state of soaring hope and euphoria.

'Oh, for God's sake.' He put a clenched hand to his closed eyes as if the struggle for self-control was slipping away from him, 'I'm asking you. No, I'm telling you, Bianca, to go to bed. Now! Before something happens which I know I'll regret. Haven't you *any* idea what you're doing to me standing there like that. Don't you *know* what I felt downstairs when I saw you and that German . . .' He broke off and took a few deep breaths.

Wolfie. The thought of him was enough to dismiss any dream. And the recollection of that wet slobbering mouth . . . She remembered the nausea she had been feeling and suddenly put her hand to her mouth.

'Oh, Daniel, I'm going to be sick.' And she rushed back into the hall, finding the door of the bathroom more by luck than by conscious effort. And sick she was—hideously, ignominiously, so that when the spasm was past she leaned with her head against the washbasin, utterly spent.

And it was the last straw that Daniel behaved like the most tender of nurses, holding her forehead while she retched, wiping her face with a cool damp cloth when she had finished, then helping her to her feet and leading her towards the bedroom.

'Oh, Daniel.' She felt giddy. 'I'm so ashamed.' Tears of self-pity streaked down her cheeks. 'But I think it must have been the prawns at dinner.'

'The prawns?' He returned from the bathroom with a glass of water in which two Alka-Seltzers were frothing, pushed it into her hand and stood by while she drank it. 'What did you have downstairs?' When she had drained the glass she offered it to him and lay back on her pillow trying to collect her thoughts.

'I had the same drink you gave me. Didn't you say it was called Mahé shandy. Only, the next ones tasted different.'

'Hmm.' He was looking at her with a very narrowed expression which she couldn't understand but suddenly her arms reached up towards him.

'Kiss me, Daniel.' A sob forced itself from her lips. 'Then I can go to sleep. I can't bear it when you hate me.'

'Oh, Bianca.' He shook his head while a faint smile turned up the corners of his mouth. 'If only I could hate you.' He bent down, and put his lips very gently to hers. 'Go to sleep, my darling.' And almost instantly, she did exactly that.

CHAPTER TEN

IT was early when Bianca woke, the sun was just rising over the horizon and the room was bathed in a soft rosy glow. If she moved her head slightly on the pillow she could see the white net at the windows moving in the lightest of spice-scented breezes while more distantly the crash of waves was insistent.

She turned in the wide bed, feet and legs searching for coolness in the smooth sheets, and paused when her eyes rested on Daniel, relaxed in sleep on the other bed, his bare chest rising and falling with his even breathing. Her heart was suddenly hammering in her throat, hammering with an insistent longing to get up and slide her hands over that smooth brown body. She knew it would feel warm, like silk under her fingers, and her whole body tingled with that knowledge.

She sighed but there was no despair in the sound. Something had happened last night, she couldn't remember what it was but she knew life was less hopeless than it had been. She sighed again, burrowed deeper into the bed and as her head moved she caught sight of the cream dress, the one she had been wearing last night, spread out on a chair at the far side of the room.

Recollection flooded back and she sat up with a gasp, hardly surprised that her face was burning. She never used that chair to deposit her clothes when she took them off. It didn't seem ridiculous that she could use a word like never when they had been there only two nights. Then her fingers slid down over the ripe curve of

173

her breast, over the low-cut nightdress with a tiny ribbon bow on each shoulder holding it in place. Bianca lay back on her pillow and groaned, then held her breath as Daniel stirred and turned over. When the deep breathing resumed, she relaxed, allowed her brain to start working again and details of all the things she would have preferred to wipe from her mind returned.

She could only suppose that after her ghastly bout of sickness last night she had passed out completely, that Daniel had finished the job of nurse by removing her dress and putting her to bed. Just like a baby. The thought drove away all ideas of sleep and after a few moments, taking infinite pains against making a sound, she swung her feet out of bed and on to the floor.

For a long time it was a pleasure just to stand there looking down at him. A pleasure and a penance because it was impossible to yield to the temptation of moving her fingers over the sprinkle of dark hair on his chest— she knew if she did that the next urge would be to lie down on the bed beside him, to stretch her body the length of his. The hammering of her pulses increased as he stirred in his sleep, he frowned and emotions chased each other across his features before he settled again into the deeply breathing pattern and she was able to make her silent escape to the bathroom.

It was bliss to feel the warmth of bathwater washing away the final recollection of the ghastly happenings of the previous night, to clean her teeth several times and to drink three glasses of cold fresh water. When she had finished, her body scented with some exotic essence, one of Fantasque's most recent introductions, she slipped on her nightdress and tiptoed back to the bedroom.

This time she couldn't risk the indulgence of standing looking down at him while he slept, but crept back into bed, pulling the light cover over her. She had had no intention of going back to sleep, but that is what she must have done because the next time she opened her eyes she found that she in her turn had been the object of study while she had been unconscious of the fact.

Daniel was lying much as he had been, only now his head was sideways on the pillow and his dark eyes were looking at her with a serious intensity which caused an immediate throb of emotion deep in the pit of her stomach. For a long time they lay, simply looking at each other; Bianca feeling the colour in her face ebb and flow, the agitation in her pulses reach a crescendo then settle down to a fierce impetuous rhythm.

'Bianca.' In his voice when at last he spoke she sensed all the hot response she herself was experiencing, which was causing a tightness across her heart, handicapping her breathing. And that was not helped by the way he quite suddenly threw back the cover and stood up. Hastily Bianca averted her eyes, uncertain . . . But when he spoke in the lazy, amused way that told her he knew only too well what she was thinking, she felt it was safe to look at him as coolly as she could make it. Which was not all that cool, but at least he *was* wearing pyjama trousers, black with some red piping she could see without looking directly at them.

'You slept well?' There was still that secret amusement in his voice, a note that made her go hot and cold all over. Then hot again she decided as she tried to catch her breath.

'Yes.' She began to ease herself into a sitting position, remembered how revealing her nightdress was and changed her mind. 'I slept very well. And I'm feeling fine.' She blushed. 'It will be a long time before I eat any more prawns. And that's a pity for I do like them.' She tried a faint smile which she thought might be encouraging, and was irrationally disappointed when she saw him frown, then rasp his fingers across his chin.

'You needn't, avoid prawns, I mean.' Abruptly he turned away from her. 'What upset you last night was the alcohol.'

'Alcohol.' Her eyes were wide with astonishment. 'But . . . What . . . ? I had only two glasses of wine. Surely that amount wouldn't upset me? Not to that extent—I really felt quite ill. Giddy. Sick. Unless, do you mean the wine was off? But you didn't . . .'

'No, not the wine.' He spoke so abruptly that she felt crushed—just when she had wakened up feeling fairly happy—but he went before she had time to feel indignant. 'Your friend Wolfie . . .'

'Your friend,' she said swiftly, determined above all things that he should understand just how she felt about that particular man.

'Let's just say Wolfie,' he grinned suddenly, his teeth showing even whiter than usual against the faint shadow of beard. 'He and his friends apparently thought it a great joke to spike your drink. After you had gone to sleep,' even without his eyes on her she couldn't have prevented the wave of colour that enveloped her, 'I went downstairs and had a word with the barman. He remembered the group as they were particularly noisy last night. Apparently they have been using the hotel for the past few days and there have been some thoughts about banning them as they have been annoying the residents. Anyway, I think I can say that from now on they'll be going elsewhere for their drinks and evening entertainment.'

'Oh . . .' Her eyes searched his face trying to determine whether she as well as the group of Germans was the subject of his anger, but when there was no sign that she was, it was possible for her to relax a little. 'I—I suppose I should have known. I *did* say I thought the drinks tasted strange.'

'Well, it wasn't your fault. It was mine as much as yours— I should have been more aware of what was happening. But from what I was able to discover afterwards I think you must have had the equivalent of several large vodkas mixed in with your Mahés. In fact,' he gave her a dry glance, 'you drank enough to put lots of people under the table. You must have quite a head.' He raised an eyebrow. 'And you say you have no hangover.'

'None. I think those Alka-Seltzers must have cured me. But . . . I never drink spirits so . . .' Disturbed by the expression in his eyes she allowed her voice to trail away. 'If I hadn't been feeling so miserable I might . . .' To her dismay he turned away, walking towards the bedroom door.

'I'm going to ring down for some tea. Would you like some?' He paused with his hand on the doorknob and looked back at her.

'That would be lovely.' She spoke in a low voice in which there was a hint of defeat, a hint which he at once picked up and tossed aside with a grin.

'Don't move. While we're waiting for the tea to come I'm going to have a shave. After that,' the look he gave her was long, languorous and did crazy unpredictable things to her heartbeats, 'we've a lot to talk about.'

When he had gone Bianca slipped down into the bed again, as much because her legs were too weak to allow her to get up as that she had had specific orders to the contrary. And it was only too easy to allow her imagination to take her along an idyllic path, the verges scattered with primroses and winding away towards some distant never-never land.

But Daniel was back before she knew it and she tried not to be affected by him, naked but for the brief royal-blue towel tied, rather insecurely she thought, round his waist while he towelled his upper torso vigorously with another. He didn't speak, hardly seemed to glance at her but she suspected that he was as vibrantly conscious of her as she was of him. And even looking at him was an intermingling of bliss and torture.

When the knock sounded from the outer door he did look at her, but seemingly only to communicate his satisfaction that tea had arrived, and she had a few moments alone to try to compose herself. Why should she imagine that things were going to be wildly different? He returned with a small tray which he put down on the table beside her bed while he hooked a chair with his bare foot and pulled it up close.

He frowned with concentration while he poured the tea but the frown eased as he handed the cup to her. Much as she would have liked to try, Bianca knew it was impossible to drink tea in a recumbent position, and sat up with an air of uncaring sophistication. The touch of his fingers started off the throbbing again, not that it had gone, but it began to regenerate simply because it was impossible for her to ignore that potent male body just on the fringe of her vision.

And while she dare not look at him, she could not ignore the fact that he was watching her with an intensity that burnt through the flimsy covering about her body. Bianca felt her precarious grip on self-control begin to slip, and her breathing became more fevered until at last she turned thrusting the cup back into his hands.

His eyes narrowed as he placed two cups carefully

back on to the tray, and then he took both her hands in his, raising them to his mouth and kissing them.

'Now,' he spoke with gentleness and a kind of finality, a great easing of spirit as if sensing that the storms were behind them, 'say to me again, what you said last night.'

'Last night?' She was puzzled and in any case could not think with the imprint of his lips on her fingers. 'Last night?' It was impossible to be aware of anything but this languorous tenderness creeping through her body.

'Yes.' His hand moved, circling her neck, and one finger stroked tantalisingly over sensitive skin. 'Last night.' A flash of humour lit up his eyes so that for an instant fires seemed to sparkle in their darkness. 'Before I—' his eyes drifted down over her barely concealed bosom, '—got you to bed.' Her confusion was no reason for him to ease his masterful scrutiny, in fact he seemed to take positive delight in the colours and expressions which chased themselves across her face. 'Remember, Bianca?' And to underline the insistence of his tone he leaned closer to her so that she could smell the clean coolness of him, and a drift of spicy aftershave touched her nostrils. And then she remembered.

'Kiss me, Daniel.' All pretence at modesty was abandoned, was replaced by an instant coquetry. She released herself from his grip and settled back against the pillow where she lay gazing up at him. She was aware of her hair spread out seductively over the white cotton and if she had been ignorant his eyes would have told her how beautiful it looked. 'Kiss me, Daniel. Then I can sleep.' Her hands reached out and touched the wide chest, finding it silky and warm as she had known. He shook his head, gave a husky laugh and leaned closer, so that their lips just touched.

'Have you always told such lies?'

The question, uttered softly against her cheek, the faint rasp of his newly shaven chin as he dropped incredibly light, tantalising kisses on her lips, on her throat and shoulder, brought her out of a half world of sleep with a murmur of pleasure. Her arms reached out to him, holding him where his mouth could most easily begin to pull her along that path which offered such an intensity of pain and joy. The lids which were settled over her eyes opened dreamily, lips curved into a smile at the sight of that dark head so close to her.

'Lies?' She couldn't even think what the word meant. Nothing mattered only this languid but quickening surge of torment in her veins. 'Lies?' She asked again, but without insistence.

'Lies.' Frustratingly his mouth moved from her breast and she looked up indignantly into the sun's filtered rays to see him leaning over her, hands on the pillows supporting him as he gazed down at her with a teasing expression on his face. He caught the hand that came up to trace a path across his chest, imprisoning her fingers against the dark curling hair then moving it to where she could feel the fierce impatient rhythm of his heart. 'You feel what you are doing to me?'

Bianca laughed and hoped his eyes would miss her increased colour.

'I can't think of any lies I've told you.' Which wasn't true, only they seemed not to matter now.

'One *lie* I just disproved a short time ago.'

'Oh, that one.' She pouted and turned her head away on the pillow. 'That was just pride.'

'Isn't that what's been wrong all along?' He sighed and laid his head beside hers, turning her face with a forceful hand so that they were very close. 'My pride, certainly.'

'Oh, Daniel.' A shuddering sigh escaped her mouth as she was forced to remember everything that had happened, and tears stung her eyes as she thought of what they might have lost. 'Oh . . . Daniel.'

'You know.' He kissed her eyes then, savouring the faint saltiness on the lashes, 'Last night, when you were dancing with Wolfie, you almost drove me mad with jealousy.'

'And what about me?' she protested. 'Don't you think that I was jealous?'

'If I had known that you were . . .' He smiled, linked his hands about her waist and pulled her close. 'If only I had known. Can you believe, I was never so uncertain of myself as I have been in the last few days. Since I came rushing back from Luxemburg a day early to find you running out on me.' Suddenly all the lightness in his face, in his voice disappeared as the darkness of recollection assailed him again. 'Why, Bianca? My darling, why?'

'Because—' she caught her voice on a half sob and stopped, unable to go on.

'Was it *really* because of what had happened all those years ago? Did it still hurt so much that you wanted to keep on paying me back?' He sighed, allowing her to sense his sadness.

'No, of course it wasn't.' Her laugh was more than a little soggy. 'Of course it wasn't.' She put her arms round his neck, comforting him as one might a small child. 'But that time at the airport. *That* really was to pay you back.' She giggled. 'I enjoyed that. And seeing it next day in the paper . . .'

'Remind me to do something about that some time. That really made me very angry.'

'Yes, I know. Freddie told me . . .' Everything Freddie

had told her flashed back into her mind and she stopped abruptly.

'Go on.' His voice was silkily insistent. 'When did you and Freddie have this intriguing conversation?'

'On Thursday.'

'Last Thursday?' He levered himself up on one elbow, looking down at her with a strange expression.

'Yes.' She hesitated, unwilling even then to ask questions the answers to which she might find unacceptable. 'Did you see her, Daniel? When you were in Luxemburg, I mean.'

'Yes, I did.' He frowned down at her and abruptly changed the subject. 'Where did you meet her, Bianca?'

'She called at my office.'

'Go on.' The eyes glittered down at her, and she noticed his mouth was a thin hard line. 'Why? Why did she come to see you?'

'She came,' Bianca drew in a shuddering sigh, 'to tell me . . . Oh, Daniel, why did you see her when you were in Luxemburg?'

'Why?' He shrugged. 'I don't think there was any reason. I just happened to meet her in the hotel dining-room. The crews often stay there, it's near the airport you see and I . . .' His frown was perplexed. 'Surely you're not telling me that Freddie called to tell you that she and I had been meeting each other by arrangement. She was, incidentally, with the first officer she's been living with off and on for the last few years.'

'Wh-What? But you and she . . .'

'Oh, we were friendly once upon a time. More than friendly, perhaps, but it was always casual and it ended when she met Lars Peterson and set up house with him. Between times she rings me when she needs a shoulder to cry on. That's what happened the night I brought her

to your sister's party. But surely . . . surely Bianca that
didn't turn you so much off the idea of marrying me. Did
it?'

'Of course not. If it had been just that I would
probably have thrown things at you but . . . it was the
other thing she said that made me want to run.'

'Tell me.' His arms were comfortingly warm.

'She said that you had no intention of turning up at the
wedding on Saturday. That you were going to pay me
back for making such a fool of you at the airport that
day.' This time the sobs could not be stilled and he held
her gently, murmuring endearments against her cheek
until she regained control. After that he dried her eyes
tenderly with a corner of the sheet.

'Don't cry any more, Bianca. I don't want to have to
swim for it.' The flicker of humour was very soon gone
and she heard the grimness in his voice as he used a very
uncomplimentary word about the stewardess. 'But how
could you believe such a thing? Do I seem such a brute
that I would do that to anyone?'

'I suppose,' she shivered a little which had the bonus
of making him pull her even closer, 'I suppose since . . .
the last time, since Simon, I've always had an inferiority
complex. Maybe I couldn't believe that someone like
you could be really in love with someone like me.'

'Oh, Bianca.' He groaned and put his cheek on hers.
'My darling, what have I done to you?' Then with a
change of mood he put his hands on her shoulders and
shook her lightly. 'You little idiot. Don't you ever look
in the mirror for heaven's sake? Have you no idea just
how beautiful you are? Don't you know how I felt when
we walked through the dining-room tonight and every
head in the room turned to look at you? Oh I admit, part
of that was the frock, but essentially it was you. You, my

love, are a knock-out and there's no place on earth I'd rather be than lying here on this bed with you. *You* have an inferiority complex! Then how do you think I feel?'

And that question while not requiring an answer was a very satisfactory one to consider. Only not right now for Daniel was already asking more questions.

'I'm trying to get the complete picture, my sweet,' she thought she might even grow to like that endearment, 'so tell me what happened next?'

'I made up my mind,' it would have helped if the story had sounded less improbable, 'that if anyone was going to be left standing at the registrar's office it wasn't going to be me, so that was why I booked the holiday to the Holy Land.'

'Holy Cow!'

'Don't mock. Anyway, as I was saying,' she caught hold of his hands which were making it impossible for her to follow a coherent train of thought, 'by the time we had arranged for our wedding I decided I was going to be as far away as possible, but of course that's when you arrived back a day early.'

'And do you really think I would have been prepared to accept that as the last word on the subject? Didn't you expect me to be waiting to pounce the moment you got back to the country.'

'I'm afraid I couldn't even think of anything in the long term. Besides,' she abandoned the submissive role, pushed him back on to the pillow and leaned over him enjoying it when his hands reached out and twisted themselves in her hair which fell like a curtain on each side of her face. 'Don't forget I thought you had abandoned me. The last thing in my mind was that you *really* wanted to marry me.'

'I've wanted, if not to marry you, at least to—' he

allowed a hand to brush against her breast and linger before he went on, 'to be in this present—' he stilled her rapid breathing with his mouth, 'in this present . . . situation since that party at Lex's. And knowing what kind of relatives you have I consider that very magnanimous.'

'Don't boast,' she said softly, leaning closer to him so that their lips could touch then laughed with unabashed triumph when he pulled her fiercely down on top of him. 'And when you appeared at the front door instead of the taxi-driver the only excuse I could think of was the one I used. I was in no mood to be jilted a second time. You ask why I believed Freddie. I might just as well ask you why you believed me.'

'Because, my darling, I know Freddie is the most unreliable woman in the world. And,' his voice hardened marginally, 'when we get back home and I'm in a slightly less indulgent mood than now she's going to wonder just what has hit her. I'll flay her alive. I could see the other night that she and Lars were in the middle of one of their periodic rows and she may have thought she had nothing else to do but whisk me over to act as a buffer.' He smiled faintly. 'I *thought* she was a bit stunned when I told her we were getting married on Saturday. But what a reaction! I didn't know she was that much of a hellcat. Yes,' he spoke as if he were turning over various appealing possibilities in his mind, 'dear Freddie is going to rue the day . . .'

'You haven't said why you believed me . . .' Bianca persisted.

'I shall always believe everything you say,' he teased then he grew serious. 'Oh, Bianca,' he groaned, sighing as he relaxed on to the pillow beside her, gazing into her eyes. 'A moment ago you mentioned Simon and I suppose it all goes back to that. We've never spoken much about him, that probably says something about my sense of guilt. Ever since we met I've been tortured by the thought of what I did to you all those years ago. Oh I was quite confident that I had been right in protecting you from your own actions but would *you* believe that? Was it possible that you were still hankering after him? Combine that with the way I fell almost instantly in love with you.' His brief laugh was not entirely amused. 'You know at thirty-four, going on thirty-five that's quite an experience for a man. I couldn't think of anything but you, I longed for you all the time we were apart. Remember, I told you that you had knocked my diary all haywire? That's the effect you had on me.' He put up a hand and brushed a coppery strand back from her forehead, and smiled when he felt the tremor run through her body, then continued.

'So you see, my darling, when I came back from that trip unexpectedly and found you all packed and ready to fly, then it all seemed utterly reasonable. I was torn apart with jealousy of course. Furious with you that you should prefer someone like Simon to me, but then women are never sensible on these matters. That,' he laid his cheek tenderly against hers, 'is one of the reasons I didn't discourage Martine when I met her on the beach. She soothed my bruised male feelings. And besides there was always the chance that you might suffer some of the pangs of jealousy that were tormenting me.'

'I did,' she said with feeling, and her answer held a hint of reproof. 'But you needn't have been jealous of Simon. Although I'm glad you were, of course,' she added with a contrariness which she considered entirely justified. 'But it was all such a long time ago. It's just occasionally something happens to bring it all back. Like that day at the airport . . .' Remembering, she gave a little giggle. 'When I saw you, found myself sitting next to you, all the old feelings boiled over. I felt so indignant that I, an innocent eighteen-year-old living alone in London for the first time—'

'You're breaking my heart—' An arm snaked threateningly round her waist.

'—Should be made so miserable by a man old enough to know better. Do you know,' indignation made her voice rise as further recollections hit her, and she rose on one elbow so that she could stare accusingly down at him, 'do you know that you accused me of being pregnant!'

'No,' he seemed suitably abashed, 'did I?'

'You were an absolute *brute!*' Her voice began to quiver but she refused to give in so easily and turned her head away so that her amusement was hidden as she collapsed on to the pillow.

'I'm sorry, my darling.' At once he was all concern, putting a finger beneath her chin, turning her head round to him. 'I'm sorry.' Then when he realised that the tremors were caused by laughter rather than tears his expression relaxed, and he waited till the spasm subsided before he leaned across to brush his mouth provocatively against hers. 'No, I'm not. I'm not the least bit sorry. You're trying deliberately to provoke me for some reason of your own.' The corners of his mouth turned up as he allowed his fingers to trickle down her neck, over her shoulder.

'But still,' he seemed reluctant to leave the subject of Simon just yet, 'you must have been in love with him at one time, otherwise you wouldn't have been planning to marry him. Would you?' His eyes were very dark and watchful.

Bianca, who was finding it increasingly difficult to think clearly, tried to concentrate her mind on finding an answer to his query. It was easy for her to know that in those far off days she hadn't had the least idea of what love was all about, but how to explain that to him? Except by the most simple of statements.

'Then,' she shook her head slightly, in disbelief at her own naïvety, 'then, I couldn't have been able to imagine I could feel like . . . this.' A faint colour rose in her cheeks, and her eyes reflected the exquisite emotions which were invading her senses. 'Until I met you, Daniel, I hadn't even the vaguest notion what love was like.'

'Darling.' His voice was suddenly husky. 'And I . . . I couldn't believe that when I loved you as I did that you could be completely indifferent. That's why I decided to take the risk of forcing you to marry me. I thought that given time I would *make* you forget Simon.'

'Daniel.' She smiled, put up a hand to stroke his cheek. 'Simon was forgotten long ago. You must believe me. In fact, I've often been grateful that something stopped me doing anything so unutterably foolish as marrying at eighteen. I'm *glad* you did what you did.'

'You could have fooled me, darling,' he smiled a little wryly. 'When I found myself at the airport with that book in my hand . . . Remind me to tell you some day just what John Crabtree of the *Globe* said to me afterwards.'

Bianca laughed. 'I didn't mean that to happen. I felt a bit mean about it when Elspeth showed me the picture in the evening paper.'

'You loved it. You know you did.'

'Well . . .' She wrinkled her nose in his direction. 'Let's say it got it out of my system once and for all.'

'In that case, I'll forgive you. If you'll forgive me . . .'

'But I've already told you . . .'

'No, not about Simon. For what I told you about Lex. I intended that you should never know about him, it was a promise I had made to myself when you said you would marry me, then at the first sign of crisis all those wonderful promises, the ones that made me feel so self-righteous, were thrown to the wind.'

'I don't think you were telling me anything I didn't suspect already.'

'I shouldn't have done it, but it was the only weapon I had, the only thing I could think of on the spur of the moment. The very thing I had sworn to protect you from. And how I longed to protect you.'

'Well, I'm rather glad you did. Otherwise, who knows, at this very moment I might have been standing outside the walls of Jericho. Or swimming in the Dead Sea.' Suddenly her teasing manner grew more serious. 'Oh, Daniel, after this we mustn't have any secrets from each other. They cause so many misunderstandings. Never.' She became more urgent, and abandoned the submissive role, pushing him back on the pillow and hardly protesting when his hands reached out, twisting themselves in the curtain of her hair. 'Promise me, Daniel.'

He smiled up at her in a way that made her heart bound wildly. 'You can get me to promise you everything while we're up on this cloud. I'm in no mood to refuse you anything.' His gentle teasing made her smile then gasp as with one practised powerful sweep of his arms he had reversed their positions so that she was lying beneath him. 'Not while I have this idea that you're little short of perfect. I might just,' he rubbed his nose on hers and grinned, 'change my mind.'

'But don't they say,' her arms linked themselves about

his neck holding him where their hearts were throbbing close to each other, 'that practice makes perfect.'

'Yes.' He whispered the words against her mouth. 'I have heard that and I've already decided I've never had a more apt pupil. Ouch!' He caught the fingers that pretended to scratch his cheek, imprisoning them against the soft curve of her breast where they could both feel the excitement of their pulses. 'But before we test out that theory, tell me the rest of the story.'

'That's all there is to tell except—' she sighed '—there were one or two things that didn't quite add up. Perhaps if I had been thinking clearly I would have realised there were several questions I should have asked.' She wrinkled her brow realising that only now were the pieces finally dropping into place. 'This holiday must have been booked several weeks ago. And yet, if you weren't going to turn up, why?'

'Correct. I made the booking when you decided on the wedding date. Next query.'

'Why buy an obviously expensive engagement ring when you've no intention of marrying the girl?'

'Exactly. And to think of how I broke my neck rushing round to your flat so I could dazzle you with my present.'

'Oh, and Daniel,' she suddenly remembered the small package in the bottom of her case, 'I have a present for you.'

'Later,' he said lazily. 'And for you, I have earrings to match your ring.'

'Oh, Daniel,' she almost wailed. 'You're making me feel awful.'

'Good,' he said equably.

'But it was so confusing.' She returned to the story. 'I knew you weren't going to marry me. But when I said I wasn't going to marry you, you said I must or else. That was more confusing still. So you see it was all quite logical.'

'Oh, Bianca,' he laughed, deeply, infectiously so that she smiled in sympathy although she was not quite certain why. 'If that's you when you're being logical, I'm looking forward to hearing you when you're being feminine and utterly irrational. Pray continue, my darling.'

'But then,' she frowned, 'I couldn't think why you didn't mind me keeping my job on. Then I decided that you didn't want to be responsible for me being on the dole if I couldn't get another job.'

'So,' he twisted a strand of her hair round her finger and frowned at it, 'you think that deep down I'm a male chauvinist.'

'Like all men.'

'Tell me,' he said menacingly, 'where did you get all your experience of men?' Then without waiting for a reply he returned to their earlier theme. 'I didn't want to ask you to give up your work unless that was what you wanted to do. But I do find the idea of your staying at home all day fairly appealing so whenever you make the decision, that's all right by me. Besides, when we find the kind of house you like you'll probably have enough to do at home.'

'Then,' she breathed against his cheek, 'you're not too sorry about how things worked out?'

'Not *too* sorry,' he assured her. 'In fact I think my plan worked out very well in the end. If I hadn't forced you to marry me then I should just have had to bring forward my abduction plan. But that would have presented further problems. The only thing I can say is,' his mouth so close to hers was encouraging all those impatient sensations which she realised she had no need to control, 'it was all right on the night. Or,' his laugh was deep and husky, 'in this case, in the morning. Wasn't it?'

'Mmm.' It heightened her trembling excitement to tease him by appearing to consider. 'Well . . .' Then she echoed his amusement with a low gurgling sound, smiling up at him for a moment before his urgent lips stifled anything else she might have been inclined to add. And it was certainly that, she decided with a sigh of sheer gratification some time later. It was very much all right on the night. Or in the morning. And she suspected it would be all right . . . any time.